A Brief Chapter in my Impossible Life

DANA REINHARDT

WALKER BOOKS
AND SUBSIDIARIES
LONDON · BOSTON · SYDNEY · AUCKLAND

This is a work of fiction. Names, characters, places and incidents
are either the product of the author's imagination
or, if real, are used fictitiously.

This edition published 2006 by Walker Books Ltd
87 Vauxhall Walk, London SE11 5HJ

YA

177517\

adoption

2 4 6 8 10 9 7 5 3 1

Text © 2006 Dana Reinhardt
Cover illustration © 2006 Harriet Russell

The right of Dana Reinhardt to be identified as author of this work has
been asserted by her in accordance with the Copyright, Designs and
Patents Act 1988

This book has been typeset in Giovanni.

Printed and bound in Great Britain by Bookmarque Ltd, Croydon, Surrey

British Library Cataloguing in Publication Data:
a catalogue record for this book
is available from the British Library

ISBN-13: 978-1-4063-0100-7
ISBN-10: 1-4063-0100-0

www.walkerbooks.co.uk

For my daughters, Noa and Zoe

one

LOOK AT US. A family of four. Seated around the dinner table. Someone asks: "Pass the couscous." The son. The younger of the two children, he has a mop of sandy blond hair the girls in his class find excuses to touch. The older sister pretends to spit in the couscous before she slides it over to him. He rolls his eyes. The parents don't notice. They're unusually quiet tonight. Mom is at one end of the table, Dad at the other. Here we are. We do this every night. We eat our dinner together. Isn't it perfect? Aren't we the perfect family?

Now look more closely. The mother also has that sandy blond hair, although hers is tied back in a loose ponytail, and let's face it: she probably could be more attentive to those split ends. The father doesn't have much hair to speak of and what he does have is darker, but the pictures in the hallway reveal that he was once a fair-haired boy with a suspicious glare for the camera.

Now look at the older sister. The differences don't stop at the hair. I have olive skin and almond eyes. I don't have the father's dimpled chin. I don't have the mother's husky voice. I'm a whiz in math. I can fold my tongue into the shape of a U. Did you know that the ability to do that is hereditary? No one else in my family can do that.

This is where we are all sitting, at the dining room table, eating Dad's Moroccan chicken with couscous, when my mother puts down her fork, fixes me with one of her looks, and says, "Rivka called. She wants to meet you."

Let's back up. Let me tell you about my day. When I was really little my parents used to start every morning by saying, "Let me tell you about your day." They'd go through every detail: "And then you are going to read some books, then you are going to have a nap, then Daddy's going to take you to the park to play with Cleo, then we're going to eat dinner . . ." Not exactly riveting information, but they said I had a problem with control and that I needed to feel like not every decision was being made for me. By the way, you'll notice that every decision was indeed being made for me, and telling me about these decisions wasn't giving me any real control over them, only the illusion that I had control over them. Which is kind of sneaky. Anyway. Let me tell you about my day and what preceded the Moroccan chicken and couscous and my parents dropping the bomb of Rivka on me.

School started last week. So you can probably imagine what it's like. There's a feeling like the year can go any way you want it to: teachers don't know you yet, your clothes are new, your hair is freshly cut and styled, and also Cleo's boobs got really big over the summer. I had suspected this all summer long and mentioned it to her on more than one occasion, but you know how it is hard to notice changes when they're happening right in front of you. So when we got back to school and a few of our other friends said something to her, she started to realize that maybe it really was true and maybe she should actually go to one of those old, heavily perfumed ladies in the women's intimates department at Filene's and get herself measured for a new bra because, as I mentioned, I'm pretty good at math, which includes geometry, and I can tell you with confidence that she is no longer a 32B. And then today Conor Spence, who's a total jerko jock but is also kind of hot if you like guys like that, which neither of us does, stopped and said, "Nice tits, Warner" to Cleo as we walked by him in the hallway, and she was totally mortified but also, I imagine, a little bit thrilled.

So after Cleo's boobs literally stopped traffic, we went to English, which is the only class we have together this semester. We've been friends since our diaper days. Her mom, Jules, and my dad met at the playground pushing us in those little bucket swings. They were both home with babies, bored out of their minds. They started to get together a couple of times a week and throw us on a blanket on the floor with some bright plastic toys we weren't supposed to choke on, although once I somehow managed to anyway. This is what they called a play date. And just in case you are getting any weird ideas about Cleo's mom and my dad, nothing ever happened there. Jules became great friends with Mom too, even though Mom was always working and not around for those mind-numbing afternoons of baby care. Jules would come over with Cleo for dinner whenever Cleo's dad was working late or out of town. But they never got together as couples because Dad and Mom never liked Edward. Eventually Jules had to admit that she didn't like him either, and when Cleo was five they got divorced. He moved to Arizona, remarried, and has two young kids. Cleo hasn't seen him since three Christmases ago.

* * *

In English class we're reading *The Great Gatsby*. I didn't read the chapters last night because . . . well, I guess I don't really have a good excuse other than laziness and my brother bursting in and out of my room to ask questions about *his* homework. I knew what he really wanted was to pump me for information about upper school, not about Algebra 1. Jake just made the gargantuan leap from the lower school to the upper school campus. It's an entirely new social order, and Jake is trying to figure out the food chain. All the people he's heard me talk about on the phone or with Cleo when she's over are suddenly flesh and blood to him. So he wanted to know if Stephanie Stark was that fat when she was going out with Mike Pine or whether her ballooning weight was the reason Mike dumped her for Heidi Kravitz. See? Jake needs me; that's why I couldn't get to *The Great Gatsby*. So in class I just sat there and drew in my notebook and listened to the discussion and actually wished I had done the reading because there were some things I would have liked to say. And mercifully, Mr. Nardo never called on me.

After U.S. history I had a free period. For the first month of school all the student groups have tables set up in the gym where you can go and take pamphlets (and free bite-sized candy bars) and sign up for the astronomy club or the yearbook or the mime troupe or the Pig Latin association or whatever. One thing I guess you should know about me is that I hate clubs. I was never a Brownie or a Girl Scout. From ages nine to eleven I slept with a Backstreet Boys pillowcase (I'll kill you if you ever tell anyone), but I never joined the fan club.

So my free period found me in the gym leafing through pamphlets and scarfing down bite-sized Charleston Chews looking for some clubs to join because Mr. McAdams told me that if I don't "diversify my resumé" I won't get into a good college. The obvious choice for me would be to join the math club, but I don't even need to go into the reasons this will never happen, do I? I wandered around for almost forty-five minutes and was no closer to joining a club than I was when I arrived, although I did consume a staggering amount of bite-sized candy.

It's not like I don't have interests. I like to write. I read a lot. I know almost everything there is to know about movies. I make my own T-shirts. I've always been fascinated by penguins, yet there doesn't seem to be a penguin club offering free Tootsie Pops. I guess there just isn't anything that defines me enough that I feel the need to make it official. It's like getting a tattoo. They're cool and I'd love to get one, once I come to terms with the fact that my parents would throw me out of the house, but I just can't come up with a symbol or a word or an image that says enough about who I am that I can live with it forever. But today, standing in that gym, surrounded by brightly colored Xeroxed pamphlets and miniature second-tier candy bars, I realized that there is this one thing that defines me, but there isn't a club for it and I can't tattoo it on my shoulder blade or on my ankle or on the small of my back. And I stood there through the ringing of the bell for fourth period and felt the sound ricochet inside my hollow head.

It's not like I haven't spent hours or days or weeks or even years thinking about the fact that I'm adopted. My parents never tried to hide it from me. Early on I understood that my straight dark hair, olive skin, lanky build, and left-handedness—all the things that make me different from my family, good and bad— come from my own mysterious genetic pool. A pool seems too small when you think about it. It really must be more like a sea or an ocean with an endless horizon. All that past—all the events that happened or didn't happen, all the weddings, births, deaths, secrets, triumphs, fighting and then making up or maybe not making up and then moving as far away as possible to get a new start—makes us who we are. But I don't know any of these stories from my own

13

oceanic past. I know only that all those events some-how dropped a baby at the feet of an idealistic young couple named Elsie Turner and Vince Bloom on an unseasonably snowy April day. And there I began my life as Simone Turner-Bloom.

I've thought about this a lot, as you can see, but you might be surprised to know that I've never wanted to learn anything about my real family tree. In my mind I've cut down those branches and left a bare, solitary trunk. I know no details. Except for one. Her name: Rivka.

Rivka. My parents would tell me that Rivka was young and couldn't keep me and that I was this won-derful gift, blah blah blah—all of the things you might imagine parents tell their adopted children. They never said anything like "God wanted us to have you," like my friend Minh's parents always told him was the reason they went to Vietnam and adopted him. My parents would never say anything about God because they don't believe in God. But they did say that they hadn't even thought yet about when or how to have a family, and when the oppor-tunity came to take me in, they just knew that this was the right thing to do. Rivka was part of the story before I was able to make it clear that I didn't want to know any details. Eventually they stopped using her name, but that name has rattled around my brain, knocking things loose, taking different forms, and sometimes waking me from the soundest sleep with its mysterious taste on my tongue.

When I was little, I somehow confused Rivka with Rikki Tikki Tavi, and in my mind Rivka was a sleek mongoose. Years later I reread that story to a sullen little girl named Lola who lived down the street. I babysat for her one summer. It was only then, sitting on the floor of her cramped bedroom, that I realized what must have caused me to morph Rikki Tikki's story with my own. He was swept up by a flood that delivered him to his new family, and I rode in on an April blizzard.

Sometimes I've thought of Rivka as a place, somewhere hot where your clothes stick to your back and the air smells like dust and mangoes. As I got older, Rivka became just a word to me, one with geometric shape, all angles and points. Somehow I've managed to keep myself from attaching it to a face that belongs to a woman whose hair will fall a certain way and who will have a certain kind of laugh.

When my mother says her name at the table, for a moment I can't imagine who she's talking about. It takes me a full beat even though earlier this same day I stood frozen in the gym, in my own way, thinking of her. But tonight I look at Mom with both shock and confusion. Dad reaches over and puts his hand over mine.

"Now, honey," he says gently, "let's take this slowly."

Jake looks up from his plate in that slightly spacey way of his and asks, "Who's Rivka?"

I know that if he took a moment and tried to use his intuition—Mom is speaking in her gentle mom voice, Dad is holding Simone's hand, Simone looks like she's about to puke or pass out or both—he'd piece it together. But let's not forget that Jake is a teenage boy and operates in the world without the power of intuition. I will say this in his defense: Jake has never asked any questions about my birth parents or how I arrived in this family. I was here before him. That's all that ever seemed to matter.

I can't speak. There's a swarm of bees in my head.

"I know how you feel about this," Mom says carefully. "And this, of course, is entirely your decision. But I think we should at least talk about it."

Jake still looks puzzled, like he's in Spanish class and he's translating one sentence behind the teacher. He has couscous on his chin.

"She's my birth mother, Einstein."

"Oh," he sort of mumbles, and looks both wounded and uncomfortable. I'm sorry I snapped at him.

I take my hand away from Dad's, not because I want to hurt his feelings but because I have a habit of biting my cuticles when I'm nervous.

Mom takes another stab at this: "Simone. I . . . We . . . We didn't think it would be right to keep this from you. She called, and she makes a pretty compelling case, and I promised her that I would let you know that this is an option that's available to you."

I notice that Dad hasn't eaten a bite of his dinner. This is pretty remarkable when you consider it's Dad. He rubs his palm over his bald spot. "Let's just sit with this for a little while, okay? We don't need to come to any decision tonight."

"No way."

That's all I can manage to say, and I get up and leave the table.

two

MY ROOM IS IN THE ATTIC. It took years and many battles, but eventually my parents agreed to let me move up here. We were a "family-bed" family. I slept with my parents until I was almost three, and by then Jake was in the bed too. It kind of makes you wonder when they even had time to make Jake. Gross. Okay, moving on . . . So I guess the attic just seemed too far away to my parents. But I think what finally made them give in had nothing to do with family bonding; rather, it was my passion for Eminem. They can't seem to hear the cleverness or the irony in his music; they can't even call it music. They just call it noise—misogynistic, homophobic, racist noise—and thus we find ourselves locked in the archetypal battle of the generations. (Can't you tell I've been studying up on the words for my college entrance exms, the SATs?) They somehow managed to survive the Backstreet Boys with little to no complaint, but Eminem just makes them crazy, and now I live in the attic.

I'm sitting on my bed doing my calculus homework when there's a knock on the door.

"I come bearing Fruit-a-Freeze. Coconut or lime?" Jake calls as he starts up the staircase.

He sits on the edge of my bed and holds out both bars.

"Which one do you want?" I ask him.

He glances back and forth. "Lime."

"Great," I say. "I'll take the lime."

He hands it to me and smiles. "Just so we're clear here: I really wanted the coconut."

I know he's come up here to make me feel better, and if he were a different kid or maybe a girl he'd probably try to talk about what happened at the dinner table, but for right now I'm so grateful that he's just Jake and that I can count on him to sit here and talk about anything *but* what happened at the dinner table.

"Your feet reek."

"Yeah," he says. He looks at them proudly and picks a piece of lint out of the tangle of blond hair on his big toe. He flicks it onto my bed. We sit eating our melting Fruit-a-Freezes. One thing about living in the attic is that it's seriously hot up here. Even in September.

"Are you going to the party at Darius's on Saturday?" he asks.

"How do you even know about that?" This doesn't square with what I imagined it would be like to have Jake in high school with me. He's not supposed to know about parties happening at the house of a senior. And even though I always went to senior parties when I was a freshman, I'm taken by surprise. Jake is a *boy*, and freshman boys go to freshmen-only parties. Lucky for them they all grow up to be seniors.

"I just heard about it. You know. Around school. Are you going?"

"I don't know," I say, even though Cleo has talked about nothing but this party all week. She fooled around with Darius at the very end of last year. She doesn't consider his not calling her or even talking to her on the last few days of school blowing her off because summer vacation was coming up and apparently there's some special dispensation awarded to guys who act like dicks right before summer vacation.

"Look, Jake, I've got to finish my homework. Thanks for the Fruit-a-Freeze. You're a prince."

"Can I bring my homework up here?" There's an armchair under the dormer window, with a trunk that serves as a coffee table. He nods in its direction.

"Sure."

We sit in silence for the rest of the night doing our

math problems with Coldplay's *A Rush of Blood to the Head* playing quietly on the CD player and the smell of Jake's feet wafting over us. I manage to avoid seeing Mom or Dad again until morning.

Friday rolls around, and the week has gone by without another mention of Rivka. Maybe I'm in the clear. Maybe I can will it or her or whatever this is to go away. When it starts to creep into my consciousness, I think of the vast ocean or the solitary tree stripped down to just its trunk—like meditating. Om. Om. See? Okay, I'm not naive. I don't think that I suddenly have hyper-Buddha powers that can banish my unpleasant thoughts and even the thoughts of others. I know Mom and Dad haven't dropped it. They're just giving it time. But sure enough, it comes up again on Friday night at the dinner table.

We're eating early because like I said it's Friday night and I'm seeing a movie with Cleo, James, Henry, and Ivy. It starts in an hour. So at least I have a built-in escape strategy.

This time I decide I can't just storm out of the room. I need to make my case.

"Look. You guys know my position on this. I just don't want to know anything. And it's not because I'm running from something; it's because I don't care.

You may think that I have some gaping hole in me or whatever your touchy-feely parenting books tell you, but I don't feel like I'm missing something and I don't have a longing or whatever and I just wish you would drop this." I can't believe it, but I feel my throat constricting and my eyes burning. I think I'm fighting off tears.

"Oh, honey." Mom lets out a sigh. Now she's annoying the crap out of me. "Whatever you decide is fine with us, you know that. We don't want to force you into anything. It's just that Rivka—"

"Will you just stop it! Jesus Christ!" I push my plate away from me and throw my napkin on top of it. "Can't you just leave me alone?" I'm shouting now. I know I seem irrational.

Dad and Mom exchange glances. I've lived with them long enough to read their unspoken language. They've decided to let it go tonight—both the topic and my outburst. There's an awkward silence.

Dad clears his throat. "So you guys," he says, "don't forget about the membership drive tomorrow."

Sometimes I feel like I've spent the better years of my youth at the local organic market trying to guilt shoppers into joining the American Civil Liberties Union. Mom has been on staff at the ACLU for twenty years. It was her first job out of law school, and now she's the legal director. Can you imagine going to the same office every day for twenty years? And she's still in the windowless nine-by-twelve room that she was first assigned. She thinks it's cozy.

Twice a year they have membership drives, and Dad and Jake and I are all called into service. The truth is I actually like doing it because I can get into some pretty heated arguments with opinionated shoppers, and the older I get the more skilled I am at arguing the need for things I believe in, like freedom of speech, women's choice, and gay rights. And also, I have to admit, even though right now I feel like strangling her, I'm proud of my mom.

"I'll be there," I say, "but for now I must say goodbye and good night."

I stand up.

"Wait," says Dad. "Aren't you forgetting something?" He gestures to his cheek. I roll my eyes and look over at Mom. I can't make a clean getaway without kissing them both. This isn't typical. They don't demand kisses anymore. But I know they feel sorry for me.

I kind of groan and quickly kiss Mom and then go over to Dad. He slips me twenty bucks. On the other hand, I decide, being pitied does have its upside.

* * *

The movie, by the way, totally sucks. And that says a lot about how bad it is because I'm not the most discriminating moviegoer. I like everything—sappy over-the-top dramas, gross-out comedies, pretentious art-house films that we have to take a trip into the city to see, and even gory slasher flicks. But this one took a battering ram to my low expectations, and I won't bore you with the details.

The theater is on Highway 33 a couple of miles out of town. Roxie's Diner is across the road and there's a fish market next door, which always struck me as an odd location for a fish market because you'd really have to want some fish to make the drive out here. The diner makes sense. See a movie, eat a burger with fries and a milk shake. But see a movie, buy a piece of fresh-frozen Icelandic cod? That I don't really understand.

After the movie we leave our cars in the parking lot and walk up the road a little way to a huge cornfield. I don't live in the boondocks, even though I know this is how it's starting to sound. We're only a thirty-minute drive from Boston, and as I mentioned, our town has an organic market. We also have a Starbucks, a chain bagel store, and even a fancy Asian fusion restaurant that charges twelve dollars for a spring roll.

We push our way through the stalks, which are fairly high this late in September, and find the clearing that's been our late-summer-early-fall after-movie hangout for the past few years. It's sort of chilly, and James is kind enough to lend me his flannel shirt.

I lie down on my back and look up at the stars. Cleo lights a cigarette. James lights a joint. Just so you know, this is *not* where this story becomes a morality tale about teen smoking or drug use. For the record, I think smoking is nasty, and I tell Cleo this all the time. She doesn't really smoke that much. She would never light a cigarette in the morning or even in the middle of the day. Cleo only smokes at night when she's hanging out with friends at parties or in corn-fields. As for the joint, I don't smoke pot, and it isn't because I'm a prude or because I'm judgmental or because I choose to "just say no." It's not because I'm afraid of disappointing my parents, because I've a pretty strong hunch that they smoked a lot of it in their pasts. Who knows, maybe they still do. No, I don't smoke pot because I've found it to be an extremely unpleasant experience. It immediately sends me into the recesses of my own head: I can't hold up my end of any conversation, and I fixate on things I would rather leave alone. But I have to admit I kind of like the smell and the silly side it brings out in these friends of mine.

Cleo and I met Ivy in first grade on the handball court during recess. She had a mean serve and braids down to her butt. We let James and Henry into our little circle in third grade because James was the skinny wimpy boy and Henry was the fat boy and none of the other boys seemed to want to play with either of them. The five of us became inseparable.

So much has changed since then, small changes like how Ivy's talent turned out to be acting, not handball, and how she replaced her braids with a three-inch crew cut. And how Henry grew out of his baby fat, and now the boys who used to tease him take orders from him because he's captain of the basketball team. Of course there have been bigger changes too, to all of us, complicated changes, far too many to mention. Now we all have our own lives and we aren't inseparable anymore, but we still enjoy going to the movies, gossiping about everyone else at school, the occasional joint, and hanging out in the cornfield.

"So, Cleavage"—this is Henry's new nickname for Cleo—"what's up with Darius? Has he weighed in on your weighty new friends?" Henry gestures to Cleo's boobs, which she's exhibiting proudly tonight in a T-shirt she should have retired even before this summer's growth spurt.

Ivy takes a long drag from the joint. "You're such a child, Henry."

"I kind of feel like touching them. Can I?" James leans in as if to make a grab. Now, I know that makes him sound like a big perv, but like I said, we've been friends since third grade, and besides, we all know that James is gay.

"Go for it." Cleo leans forward. He sort of pokes one and then quickly pulls his hand away. "Yep, they're the real thing."

Cleo makes a slight readjustment. "Like you would know."

"Hey, what about my turn?" Henry reaches over.

"Go fondle your own boobs."

Everyone laughs. Ivy lies down next to me and puts her head in Henry's lap.

"We're smart people, right?" Ivy asks. "Well then, tell me, geniuses, why is it that we didn't think of smoking this joint *before* the movie?"

Aside from the sound of my friends' voices and the occasional car passing out on Highway 33 and the rustling of the cornstalks in the autumn breeze, it's stone quiet out here. There's a blanket of stars in the sky. There's no moon to speak of. I feel sheltered, protected, safe. I'm sitting in this cocoon in the middle of a cornfield on the outskirts of a town I've lived in since birth with a group of friends I've known forever, and yet when James points out that I'm quiet tonight and asks if everything is okay, I just say that I'm tired and that I think I need to go home.

Cleo is spending the night. Lucky for us my parents are asleep, because she reeks of smoke and is still a little high. As is the rule in our house, I tiptoe into their room and whisper that I'm home. I always stand outside their bedroom door for at least a full two minutes listening with almost superhuman strength for the slightest rustle of the sheets or any sound that might indicate that they're engaged in . . . well, you know. See, I can't even bring myself to say it. I'm far more terrified of discovering my parents mid-act than I am of being busted for drinking.

Mom turns over and mumbles, "Hi, sweets. Give me a kiss."

I know this routine. I'm no fool. I lean in, and she takes a long, deep, and noisy sniff of me. She rolls back over. I'm clean.

She lets out a yawn. "Night-night." She's asleep again before I shut the door behind me.

Cleo and Jake are both in the bathroom brushing their teeth. He's like a little brother to her too. She's known him since he was born, and she's an only child, unless you count her dad's new kids in Arizona, which Cleo most definitely does not. In fact, she pretends that she can't remember their names, which for the record are Carly and Craig. I think Jake has always been kind of in love with Cleo, and that might freak someone else out, but I think it's sweet.

"No wonder your breath always stinks, Jake," Cleo teases him. "You're a godawful brusher. Didn't anyone ever tell you about the importance of circular motion?" She demonstrates. "See," she says through a mouth full of foamy paste, "it's all about the gums." She takes out her toothbrush and swipes his nose with it.

He pretends to be disgusted and quickly rinses his face in the sink. He has on a pair of blue and orange plaid pajama bottoms, slippers I gave him last Christmas that look like bears' feet (get it? He's in his "bear" feet), and no shirt. Jake is really starting to fill out, and he tends to walk around shirtless whenever he can get away with it.

"Good night, ladies," he says, and even though Cleo's face is covered in apricot scrub and I've just started brushing my teeth, he flicks off the bathroom light.

I'm lying in bed. Cleo shuts down my computer after checking her e-mail and then turns to me and says, "Simone, are you sure you're okay? You just seem kind of bummed out tonight."

There it goes again. That burning in my eyes. That

constricting of my throat. Why is this happening?

"Yeah. I'm fine. Just tired." I fake a yawn.

She crawls onto the futon we put down for her on the floor. "Come on, Simone. Tell me what's going on."

Now I feel myself sort of cracking inside. It's pitch black in here, and I figure I can get away with letting a few tears roll down my cheeks. There's a long silence, and I wipe my running nose on my sleeve, being careful not to sniffle. Suddenly I realize that I *am* really tired, but mostly I'm tired of pretending that this isn't bothering me.

"I'm just having a really weird week." My voice is shaky.

Cleo waits.

"My parents told me that Rivka wants to meet me." I say this knowing full well that Cleo doesn't know who Rivka is, but I can't think of what else to call her. My birth mother? The woman who gave birth to me? None of it feels right. But good old Cleo needs no explanation. She, unlike Jake, has the power of intuition.

"Wow," Cleo says. "That's heavy."

"Yeah."

"So, what do you think?"

"I don't know."

"Aren't you curious?"

Am I curious? How can I be curious? I've spent all my life fighting off that curiosity. I've locked it away. I've thrown it overboard. I've beaten it to a pulp. But here it is anyway, back from the dead. And even though I'm older and wiser and stronger, I seem to be losing the battle against it. But I'm not ready to admit this tonight to Cleo or to anyone else. I just lie there with my burning eyes open, staring at the glow-in-the-dark stars on my ceiling. They have almost no glow left in them. When you see stars in the sky, they are nothing but tiny dots. When you look at them through a telescope, they look more like little balls of light. They don't look anything like the shapes on my ceiling—the shape we learn to draw as children, with five protruding angles. But then again, the heart looks nothing like the shape we learn to draw as children either, so there you have it. I start breathing deeply, and Cleo either believes that I'm asleep or is a good enough friend to let me get away without saying anything more.

three

It's way too early in the morning for political debate, but here I am with my ACLU baseball jersey on outside the Organic Oasis.

"Do you have a moment for the ACLU? Do you have a moment for the ACLU?"

Jake and Dad have the parking lot entrance in the back, and I'm covering the sidewalk out front, where there are crates of fruit on display and bushels of fresh cut flowers. So at least it smells good out here. A few bleary-eyed shoppers stumble past me without so much as a glance in my direction. I decide that no one is in the spirit yet, particularly me, so I go inside to get a cup of fair-trade coffee.

Zack Meyers is working at the coffee counter. We haven't had any classes together, but we obviously know each other's names because there are only 198 juniors at Twelve Oaks Academy.

"Hey, Simone. You're up early."

I'm wondering if this is maybe the first time we've ever actually spoken to each other.

"Yeah, I'm trying to sign up members for the ACLU."

"Cool."

Zack has small wire-rimmed glasses and really red cheeks, and he always wears camouflage Converse high-tops to school, although I can't see over the counter to confirm that this is true when he's outside of school. He also has an earring (a small dangling lightning bolt), which is so eighties but somehow looks okay on him. He hangs around Amy Flannigan all the time. I wonder if they're going out. He takes pictures for the school newspaper. I think I've seen him playing tennis on the courts at school. And, I realize this morning, he happens to be really, really cute.

He leans on the counter. "So, what'll it be?"

"Just a regular good old-fashioned coffee. Hold the crap."

Oh, no. Did he know that by "crap" I meant the milk or foam or hazelnut syrup? I'm suddenly terrified that he thinks I meant the conversation. I try to recover:

"Why don't people just drink coffee anymore? Why does everything have to be all complicated?"

Now I'm sounding like an idiot. This is not an original or even remotely witty observation. It's not like I'm the first person to poke fun at the world of Frappuccinos and fancy coffee.

"Well, at least it keeps my job interesting. Imagine if I only poured regular coffees all day. Where's the satisfaction in that?" He hands me my coffee and smiles. I smile back. Then I realize he's waiting for me to pay because there's someone standing behind me.

I hand him my dollar twenty-five and say casually, "Thanks. See you around."

I go back outside to find a few other baseball-shirted people with clipboards. I don't recognize any of them, which leaves me wondering two things: (1) Why is it that only my mom enlists her family for membership drives? And (2) why do we have to start a full hour before anyone else?

I meet the other signature gatherers. They are volunteers, a retired couple in their sixties named Ann and Sy and a woman named Lena with short red hair who looks like she's pushing thirty. Things are picking up—more shoppers are arriving, and some are even stopping to sign up. Just for sport, I step in front of a woman who looks like she's doing everything she can to avoid contact with me.

"Do you have a moment for the ACLU?"

She stops and lets out an exasperated sigh. "No, I absolutely do not have as much as a second for the ACLU. I am sick to death of the ACLU." I feel like pointing out to her that a moment technically can be a second and that already she has given about fifteen of them. "Can't you find anything better to do with your time? Why stand out here advancing the work of an organization that is trying to tear apart this town?"

I'm not really sure what she's talking about, but I'm ready to dig in for a fight. Is this about gay marriage? Abortion? I mean, abortion is a debate I feel like I can contribute a powerful perspective to. It goes like this: I easily could have been aborted, right? I was lucky and wasn't, and I was adopted by a loving family. But I still believe in a woman's right to choose, even knowing what a close call my very existence is. This woman is talking about something else, though.

"There is history here," she tells me, and she is so angry now that she's turning red and kind of whispering and spit is flying everywhere. "You can't erase history. And more importantly, you can't erase God. No matter how much money you raise." With that she walks away.

Lena sees me looking confused and comes over.

"I've come across a few like her today. They're all pissed off because of the town seal case." She explains that she doesn't mean the aquatic mammal (this I'm sure is supposed to be a joke, but maybe I look like a child to Lena), she means the town seal, which has four quadrants with a book, a tree, a bell, and a cross. Now, I didn't even know that we had a town seal, and I would bet you anything that you'd be hard pressed to find five people in the Organic Oasis or beyond who do. But I guess that's starting to change with this case. Maybe Mom told me about it and I didn't really pay attention, but more likely she didn't tell me about it because you know how it is—she's my mom and she spends most of her time trying to extract information from me about my life. It doesn't happen the other way around.

So we have a town seal. The book symbolizes learning. The tree symbolizes growing. The bell symbolizes freedom. And the cross—well, that's obvious. The seal is on our town flag, which I guess flies above the town hall, although I have to admit I've never noticed this.

Mom stops by in the afternoon, and when I ask her about the case she points out the irony of the bell and the cross positioned next to each other on the seal. The cross, she tells me, infringes on the freedom of anyone who is not a Christian. This makes total sense. I mean, I don't believe in God and I have to live in this town too, so why should I have to live

36

with that cross in my face all the time? Suddenly I'm indignant. I totally believe in this case, and I wish I could turn back time and have an informed argument with that uptight bitch from this morning. The funny thing (well, one of the funny things is that of course I didn't even know we had a town seal, so saying that I have to live with it in my face all the time is pretty funny) is that technically speaking, Mom is a Christian. So is Dad. So, I guess, are Jake and I. Like I said before, my parents don't believe in God. I don't believe in God. We don't go to church or pray or do any of those things. And even though whenever someone asks me what I am, I say, "Nothing," my parents come from the Christian tradition: Catholic in my dad's case, Episcopalian in my mom's. And as far as I know they didn't go through any kind of ritual to erase their Christian pasts and become something else. Doesn't this mean that to the rest of the world we're Christians, no matter how we define ourselves? I guess the important thing is that having a cross on our town seal infringes on the freedom of not only those people who practice other religions but also people like my family and me. People who call themselves nothing.

Darius's party that night is kind of a bust for me. Cleo disappeared early on with Guess Who into a bedroom upstairs, and I'm bored and about to go home at the shockingly early hour of ten o'clock. I've had about half a beer from the keg; it was warm and tasted like pee. I think a day of nonstop conversation with complete strangers, many of whom were unpleasant, didn't exactly leave me in the mood for small talk. The music is loud, the bass is turned up way too high, and my head is throbbing to the beat of some awful techno trash. I know I sound like an old lady here, but it really has been a long day and the music is just unbelievably atrocious. I wander around the party with my head lowered, avoiding the throngs of people I have no interest in talking to and, okay, I'll admit it, scanning the floor for a pair of camouflage high-tops.

I'm thrilled to find James in the backyard sitting on a lawn chair.

"Hey, baby." He motions for me to sit on his lap.

"Hey."

"Why the long face?"

"I'm just beat."

"This is getting to be a theme with you."

"Okay. I'm beat, and this party totally blows."

"Speaking of totally blowing, have you seen Cleo and Darius?"

I smack him on the chest. "You are so foul."

"No, I'm just jealous."

"Why?" I ask. "You want to be upstairs with Darius in his parents' tacky bedroom?"

"No, but it would be nice if not every guy at these parties were so terminally straight. I'd like at least the illusion that I could meet someone."

"You could take me home and see if you get lucky."

Cleo drove me here, and our arrangement was that if she just happened to lose me during the party for any reason (gee, what could that be?) and couldn't find me later, she would assume that I found a ride.

We climb into James's car and I say, "Home, James." This joke somehow never gets old to me.

James drives a rattly 1988 Volvo. I think it may be louder in his car than it was at the party. He's talking about his summer at the Rhode Island School of Design again and how much cooler all the people were there than they are at Twelve Oaks and how he can't wait to go off to college in New York City and get out of this town. I know why he has this fantasy about going to college in New York. James had his first boyfriend over the summer, and Patrick is starting his freshman year at NYU. He broke up with James at the end of the program at RISD and told him that there is just too much happening in New York City and he doesn't want to be thinking about someone who lives far away.

Poor James. Darius's party was far from the anti-
dote he needed tonight for his broken heart.

When we pull up in front of my house I say, "Want to
come inside?"

"So that whole thing about me getting lucky
wasn't a joke?"

"Of course it was a joke, you homo. I want to
know if you want to come inside and eat some ice
cream and see if there's any stupid girly movie on
cable."

James takes a minute to think it over and then
takes a pass. I don't push him on it. I have a pretty
good idea of how he's feeling tonight. So I kiss him
goodbye and stand on the sidewalk in front of my
house watching the one working taillight on his
Volvo fade into the night.

four

YOU KNOW HOW THEY SAY that after women give birth, a chemical is released in their brains that causes them to forget the pain of childbirth so they're able to face it again? That's sort of what it's like for me with winter. Even though I know that the turning of the leaves is just a harbinger (one of my favorite SAT words) of the endless months of snow and slush that lie right around the corner, I just love this time of year. Our street is lined with fire-engine-red trees, and when I stand on the sidewalk, it's literally as if I am viewing the world through rose-colored glasses. I'm waiting for Cleo to pick me up for school.

She's late. Typical. When she arrives she seems totally frazzled. She has a mug of coffee in her hand—not even a travel mug, just a white porcelain mug with hearts on it that says SOMEONE IN SAVANNAH

LOVES ME—and a brush sticking out of her damp mass of curly hair.

"Hold this." She hands me the mug and shifts gears, and we're off.

She's yanking at her hair with the brush, muttering obscenities, and finally she just gives up and tosses it in the backseat. She sees me eyeing the mug.

"My grandma, obviously. But I think it pushes the boundaries of cheesy to such an extreme that it actually cycles all the way back around to cool. Don't you think?"

"I buy that."

Then Cleo launches into the daily Darius report, which mostly involves her making excuses for his poor behavior. I'm getting a little talked out on the whole Darius thing, and I don't mean to sound uncharitable or to imply that Cleo is totally self-absorbed, which she's not. Cleo's a great friend, and we've probably spent as much time talking about my situation with Rivka as we have about her situation with Darius. But there just doesn't seem to be a lot of change in the daily soap opera that is Cleo and Darius, and yet we dissect each exchange like it's a passage from *The Great Gatsby* (which I did finally read and which is a kick-ass book). Here's what's important to know: They're "going out," although he doesn't call her his girlfriend—much to her annoyance. They don't hold hands or anything like that at school because he thinks that stuff is stupid. I have to admit that I kind of agree with him on that one. And, most importantly, they haven't had sex yet. There's a lot of behavior that pushes the boundaries to the extreme, as Cleo might say, but they haven't had actual old-fashioned sex, or what they might call "intercourse" in sex ed. I'm glad because I don't trust Darius to stick around for long and I worry about Cleo getting used, but at the same time I kind of wish they'd do it because those are the details I want to hear about.

I tell Cleo about the huge fight I had with my parents last night over the Rivka Situation. They're driving me crazy. For weeks now, at every opportunity, they drop hints they think are subtle but are far from it, and I guess they got tired of me ignoring them because last night they sat me down for a talk.

I hate my parents' talks. I hate the way they look at me. Particularly Mom. She gets this attitude like she's the lawyer and I'm on the witness stand. I feel like screaming at her that even though she spends most of her time at work, she's home now, and I'm not a client or somebody she's trying to sue or even one of her volunteers spending my Saturday in her service arguing with local shoppers about the First Amendment. I'm just her daughter.

43

Dad is much easier to take in these situations, but that's probably because he sits there and lets Mom do most of the talking. Come to think of it, that can get pretty annoying too.

"All right. Fine. What?" That's how I started our talk.

"Honey," Mom said, "you know we don't like to tell you what to do—"

"Well, then don't."

"But we really think that you should at least give Rivka a call."

"See? You just did it. You just told me what to do."

"She wants to talk to you."

"So?"

Mom looked at Dad. He looked down at the floor.

"She might have things to say that are important for you to hear."

"Like what? If she had something so important to tell me, she wouldn't have waited sixteen years."

"Honey, she hasn't waited sixteen years. We've told you before that we've been in touch with her since you were born. She's always known about you. She always wanted to know about you."

"*Stop*," I shouted at her. I pulled my knees to my chest and put my head down. I didn't want to hear this. I didn't want to hear that she's been calling, that she knows that I go to Twelve Oaks, that I broke my wrist when I was five, that I was the scarecrow in the seventh-grade play. That is none of her business. I am none of her business.

When I lifted my head from my knees I saw that Dad was still looking at the floor. Suddenly it occurred to me that maybe there was a rift in this united front.

"Why don't you say anything, Dad? Why are you just sitting there?" I asked.

"I don't know, kid. This is tough for me. I hate to upset you." Mom shifted away from him on the couch. His eyes were heavy and sad. Looking at him, I could see all the hours they'd put in on this topic, and I could tell that it hasn't been easy on him.

"Well, congratulations. You managed to upset me anyway. Thanks a lot."

I picked up the remote control and turned on the television, signaling that, from my perspective, our talk had come to an end.

Mom held out a piece of paper. "Please, just take her number."

I took it partly to shut my mother up, partly because of the circles under my father's eyes, and partly because no matter how hard I try to fight this, there's that curiosity again, rearing its ugly head.

I stormed out of the living room and slammed my door a full three times just to make certain my parents could hear it. I turned the volume on my stereo up to eight, four notches higher than what is allowed in my house. I sat down at my desk, booted up my computer, and did some Internet research. Here's what I learned: Rivka's number has an area code and three-number prefix that I believe lands her somewhere on Cape Cod.

Cape Cod, Massachusetts, USA, planet Earth.

I put the number in my drawer not knowing if or when I'd ever make this phone call, but I hoped that taking the piece of yellow scrap paper into my possession was a big enough step that I've earned the right to be left in peace for a while.

After school today I have the first meeting of my new club, the Atheist Student Alliance. My guidance counselor, Mr. McAdams, tells me that this isn't going to win me a coveted spot on any of the Ivy League admissions lists and that this wasn't exactly what he had in mind when he told me I needed to get more involved in after-school activities. On the other hand, he was so excited when I told him I joined the school newspaper that he actually burst into applause. It was kind of embarrassing. The poor guy seriously needs to get a life. Okay, I know what you're thinking. So maybe my motive for joining the staff of the *Oaks Gazette* wasn't purely the love of the printed word, but I'll have you know that I'm really into being on the school paper. And this has absolutely nothing to do with Zack Meyers because I still haven't had a conversation with him as remotely involved as the one that morning at the market.

My first assignment was to write a story on this sophomore kid who won the statewide science project competition. I know that sounds boring, and if you just write a story that says here's this kid and here's what his project was and he won a $500 cash prize, that *is* boring. But what I learned in working on this article is that everyone has an interesting story to tell. This kid's father is a professor at Brandeis University, and he spent a year living in Tanzania when his dad was on sabbatical, and that's where he got the idea for the farming experiment that won him the science competition. He always had a terrible phobia of bugs, but what he learned in Tanzania was that bugs can be used for positive purposes. So this kid started experimenting with planting and using bugs in the soil, and just like that he overcame his lifelong phobia and won a $500 prize. See? The story has adventure, mystery, and triumph over adversity. My article was like a mini-biography. It was a pretty good story, and I'm sure if I had more time and more print space I could have written a lot more about this kid, who at first seems like a total geek but has a life story as interesting as anyone else's, at least as interesting as that of anyone else from Twelve Oaks.

Susan Linder was assigned to take the pictures for the article, not Zack Meyers. But what I've managed to learn in my short time at the *Gazette* through both observation and careful questioning of other staffers is that Zack and Amy Flannigan are not going out; they are just best friends who do everything together.

The meeting of the Atheist Student Alliance is taking place in the same room where I have my calculus class, which seems fitting to me because I don't see how anyone with a mathematical mind can believe in God. It just goes against logic. The group is pretty small and also pretty diverse. I mean diverse in the sense that there are kids from different grades and social circles here. There isn't a whole lot of racial or even economic diversity at Twelve Oaks, which I know is something that's always bothered my parents, and that's why ever since I was pretty young I've gone to a city-run summer camp in Boston. I've come to agree with them, and now I work there as a counselor. But looking around the room, for such a small group, there is a fair amount of diversity in here. Jasmine Booth-Gray is here. Also Minh Clarkson, my friend who was adopted from Vietnam, is here—the one whose parents have always told him that God sent him to their family. Do they know he's a member of the ASA?

Heidi Kravitz is the president, so she runs the meeting. She tells us that on Columbus Day there's going to be a rally in front of the town hall in support of the town seal and that we're going to be part of a counterdemonstration. I debate whether I should chime in that my mom is the lawyer who is bringing the case, but this is my first meeting and I don't want to look like I'm bragging or anything, so I keep quiet. We're organizing the counterdemonstration with the Young Democrats, and I'm sure if there were a Jewish Student Alliance or a Muslim Student Alliance on campus they would join us too, but there is no such thing not only because, like I mentioned, Twelve Oaks isn't exactly a beacon of diversity, but because there is a ban in our school charter against religious groups operating on campus. So there isn't even a Christian Student Alliance. I'm pretty psyched for the demonstration, and I'm just praying in my not-believing-in-God kind of way that I run into that woman from the Organic Oasis so that I can give her a piece of my well-informed mind.

Cleo and her mom are coming over for dinner tonight. Dad is in the kitchen using every bowl, knife, and kitchen utensil imaginable. Jake comes home from soccer practice (my little brother the jock) and heads upstairs for a much-needed shower. I'm sitting in the living room going through more SAT vocabulary words. I don't have to do any studying at all for the math part of the SAT, so I figure if I can give all my time over to the verbal part, then I can probably get a high enough overall score to make up for my late arrival to the world of extracurricular activities. Here's one: *insensate*. Wouldn't you think that means furious? Well, it doesn't. That is the word *incensed*. *Insensate* means having no feeling at all. Who can keep this stuff straight?

From the kitchen Dad calls out for help. He's making lasagna, and because Dad can't seem to do anything halfway, he's making the noodles from scratch. He's already kneaded and flattened the dough into long sheets of pasta, and now there's some process that involves dropping them in boiling water and then quickly plunging them in ice water. This requires more hands than Dad's two. I wonder if all this is a sign that things at work are going slowly for Dad. He's a cartoonist who does political cartoons for magazines and the *Boston Globe*. I know this sounds like he should be really funny, and Dad is a lot of things, but funny isn't one of them. He's a great cook, I'll give him that. He can kick my butt at Scrabble. He has a halfway decent singing voice. But funny? Not my dad.

I offer to help like a dutiful daughter. I wash my hands in the sink, and then we stand there side by side: first the boiling water, then the ice water.

"So what's new at school, kiddo?"

Why do parents always ask such lame questions? Adults always complain that their kids never talk to them, but if they open up conversations this way, what do they expect? I give him the stock answer.

"Not much," I say. But then I decide to take pity on him. He has flour on his nice linen shirt. "I had my first Atheist Student Alliance meeting today."

"Really?"

"Yeah."

"And how was that? Tell me about it."

So I tell him all about the meeting and the demonstration coming up, and he looks at me as if he's going to explode with pride. You'd think I'd told him I got 1600 on my SATs. Go figure.

The lasagna is now ready to be assembled. I help him build the layers.

"Have you given any more thought to making that phone call?" Dad keeps his eyes fixed on the mound of grated cheese. I'm cornered. I've let my guard down. I should have seen this coming. I've been avoiding these situations with my parents for precisely this reason. We were having a nice time. Why did he have to ruin it?

"Yeah. I have," I say. "And what I keep thinking is this: Why are you on my case about this? Why do you care about this so much? Why can't you leave me alone?" I pause. He stands motionless. "Unless, of course, you're trying to get rid of me." I say this last part knowing that it isn't true but wanting to inflict some kind of pain on Dad, to give him a small dose of what I'm feeling.

"That's crazy. Don't even joke like that. Ever." He wipes his hands on his apron and finally looks at me. I can see that I've succeeded in my mission. He looks wounded. "My job is to protect you. That's my main responsibility in this world. So it goes against my instincts to push something on you that seems to upset you so much. But I also want you to have every opportunity that's available to you. I want you to know everything about yourself that there is to know. Things that your mother and I can't help you with."

I open my mouth to speak, but my words get caught in my throat. I take a sip of water.

"But why now?"

Dad is quiet for a long time. We work side by side in silence.

"You'll have to ask Rivka that."

We put the final layer on the lasagna and it is done.

*   *   *

Cleo is in a mood when they arrive. I assume that Darius has made yet another egregious (SAT word) misstep in his behavior toward Cleo. But I don't have time to ask because we sit down to eat immediately after they arrive, which is of course half an hour after they were due.

Jules is talking about some woman from her office who may or may not be having an affair with the boss, and I stop and realize that life just never changes. Jules and Dad and Mom sit around and talk about other people in the same way that Cleo and James and Henry and Ivy and the rest of our friends do. The only difference is that the people they talk about are older and I guess the stakes are higher since it appears as if the boss and the woman from Jules's office are both married.

Cleo is quiet and won't even look at Jules. This is unusual. Cleo and Jules act more like friends than mother and daughter.

My mom studies Cleo. "Can I get you anything, honey?" Cleo has an untouched plate of food and a full glass of lemonade.

"No, thanks."

"Don't mind my daughter, Elsie," Jules says. "She's having a tantrum."

Cleo sighs and drops her fork. It's clear that she

didn't really want to talk about this at the table, but she also doesn't want Jules to have the last word.

"No, Elsie. Don't mind my mother. She's just being a selfish, unthinking, cruel, and negligent wench."

Silence. Jake pretends to wipe his mouth with his napkin to hide his big goofy grin. Did Cleo really just call her mother a wench?

Jules says to no one in particular, "Cleo's angry because Edward wants her in Arizona for Thanksgiving and I think she should go." She turns to Cleo. "And I really don't see how this makes me negligent. Your father lives in a mansion. He has live-in help. There's a swimming pool."

"See? I could fall in and drown."

"Okay, now you're just being ridiculous."

Dad cuts himself another piece of the lasagna, which I must add is really excellent.

"Cleo," he says, "it might be nice to go to Arizona. Get a little sun. Hang out with your dad. It's been a while, hasn't it? He must really miss you."

"Come on, Vince. You know Dad doesn't give a shit about me. Why are you defending him?"

Dad bristles a little at Cleo's use of the S-word. Unlike Mom, Dad is a bit of a prude in the language department. "Well, I'm not defending him. But he is your father. I just think it's important that you keep up a relationship with him."

54

"Yeah, I guess I just don't understand why you aren't having this conversation with *him* instead of me."

I'm having a weird kind of déjà vu. Here we are again, sitting around the dinner table, this time with our extended family, Jules and Cleo. Again an absent parent is disrupting our meal. Even though these parents are very much alive and out there in the world somewhere, tonight they are like ghosts hovering around us. And suddenly our dinner table feels really, really crowded.

five

THERE'S GOING TO BE ANOTHER PARTY at Darius's house (are his parents ever in town?), this time a small one, on the Sunday night before Columbus Day, which is of course a school holiday and also the day of the demonstration outside the town hall. I agree to go with Cleo even though James and Henry and Ivy are going to Rich Campbell's. Rich lives on this huge farm, and there's going to be a bonfire. I love bonfires. Who doesn't? Even so, I agree to go with Cleo because I'm a good friend. I agree to go with Cleo even though I don't think Darius likes me, which would make sense, because I definitely don't like him.

On the night of the party I go over to Cleo's to get ready. I'm also going to sleep over because I plan on not passing Mom's sniff test tonight, and Jules is always paranoid about not getting enough sleep, so she doesn't want Cleo waking her up when she gets home. I'm lying on Cleo's bed while she sits in front of the mirror trying to tame her unruly hair. She's wearing jeans and black boots and a T-shirt I made for her that says PROM QUEEN on it. Just in case you haven't picked up on my brand of humor, the shirt is supposed to be ironic. She puts on some lipstick that's barely noticeable, and when she turns around she looks beautiful, elegant even.

"How do I look?"

How can she not know how she looks? For Cleo, things like beauty and elegance and grace come naturally. I can remember when we used to take ballet together, and at the recitals, when it came time to curtsy, she would walk right to the center of the stage with her perfect posture and her Shirley Temple curls and the world just stopped. But for the life of me, I could never get that moment right.

"You look amazing," I say. "On the other hand, I look like a total slob."

Cleo cocks her head and checks me out. I can see her mind working. She recognizes a challenge, and she's gearing up to meet it. Where I see a slob, she sees potential. Where I see nothing special, she sees a blank canvas. I'm wearing cords and a button-down oxford. She goes over to her dresser and pulls out a black long-sleeved shirt with a V-neck, made of some kind of spandex blend.

She throws it at me. "Put this on."

By spandex I don't mean to make it sound like some shiny, cheesy workout wear or anything. It's just a long-sleeved T-shirt with some cling in it, and when I put it on I have to admit that it's a drastic improvement. Unlike Cleo, I don't have gigantic boobs. I don't even have medium-sized boobs. But somehow this black shirt gives the impression that there is more there than meets the eye.

Cleo looks pleased. "I don't know why you insist on hiding your assets. You're hot. If only you could see that."

She's right. I don't see it and I don't believe that anyone other than Cleo sees it, and anyway, Cleo is probably just trying to be nice. I'm fine. I'm passable. There are other things just as important as being hot, like being smart and responsible and a good listener. But it never seems like these things matter to guys, and isn't that what we're talking about here?

I take another look in the mirror. Cleo's right. Even I can see that this new look brings out something in me, something that has nothing at all to do with my grades or my listening skills.

The party is already in full swing when we arrive. Everyone is hanging out in the living room listening to more of Darius's horrid music. To his credit, when we walk in Darius stands up and kisses Cleo in full view of his friends. She looks like she could die right there. He gives me a kind of awkward hug and offers to get me a drink.

"Beer? Wine cooler? Something stronger?" The taste of the beer from Darius's last party is still fresh in my memory. I tell him I'll take vodka mixed with whatever kind of juice he has in the house. Cleo doesn't take anything. She's the designated driver.

"Someone's in the mood to party," she says to me as Darius walks over to the bar. I figure I've earned it. It's been one of those weeks. You know the kind. A disappointing grade on a French test I really studied for, a stupid fight with my brother, a comment made about me by someone I hardly even know, which I learned about through the Twelve Oaks grapevine, where information travels at the speed of light. It was this girl in one of my classes named Brianna, and she said I was full of myself. It bothers me, even though I can't believe I'm letting someone whose name is *Brianna* get to me, because I really don't think that I am full of myself. Or does thinking you're not full of yourself show that you have such a high opinion of yourself that you actually *are* full of yourself? Now I'm getting confused.

Anyway, it was one of those weeks. And do you notice how I'm pretending as if that yellow scrap of paper with the Cape Cod phone number written on it isn't burning a hole in my desk drawer?

I take a huge gulp of the drink Darius brings me and then cringe. Not because of the burning sensation of the alcohol but because of the nasty flavor of whatever Darius mixed it with.

He looks at me apologetically. "All I could find was this ginseng stuff my mom drinks. She's a total health freak."

I'm not sure how this accounts for the impressively stocked bar, but I figure maybe his dad is the big boozer and stays home getting drunk while his mom goes off on her yoga retreats. Then I realize that of course I don't know anything about Darius or his family, and I wonder for a minute what people who don't know me come up with to account for my dark hair and olive skin in a family full of pasty blondes.

I decide not to cling to Cleo all night—she really wants to be (and be seen) with Darius. And besides, I should mingle because I certainly don't want to appear as if I'm full of myself. So I go over and sit on the sofa next to Tim Whelan.

He has a beer in his hand, and I wonder if drinking that stuff actually makes your breath smell of pee, but I don't think that would be an appropriate conversation starter. Instead I ask how his team did today because I know enough about Tim Whelan to know he plays varsity soccer.

"We did pretty well. I mean, we won and that's great, but we should have played a better game. We were weak on defense." Then he looks at me with this funny expression. "But you don't really care about this at all, do you?"

Now I'm totally paranoid. Does everybody in the entire school know me as the girl who is full of herself?

"Relax," he says. "I'm kidding. It's just that I've never seen you at a game or anything." He smiles at me.

Oh. Now I get it. Tim isn't trying to be rude. This is his weird way of *flirting* with me. It must be the shirt. I take a closer look at him. He's kind of cute even though I don't usually like the athletic types. It's October and not exactly sultry out, but he's wearing baggy cargo shorts, a blue fleece pullover, and a pair of Tevas. He has big brown eyes, a large forehead (which is a nice way of saying that his hair seems to be receding prematurely—very prematurely), and a small scar just above his upper lip. We sit there for a long time drinking our foul-tasting drinks and talking about soccer—he thinks Jake will make varsity next year—the school paper, some of the teachers we both have, and that horrible movie I saw last month, which he thought was pretty funny. I'm starting to get a little bit buzzed, and I feel sort of warm inside, and even the music isn't bothering me anymore. I don't even know how much time has gone by. And by the way, Tim's hand is on my knee.

He stands up and stretches.

"Let's go refresh our drinks." He leans down and looks in my cup, then leans in a little closer to take a whiff. "What the hell is in there?"

"Ginseng."

He looks confused.

"I think I'll go for a wine cooler this time."

We get drinks, and then he suggests we go sit outside. Now, I'm not stupid. Full of myself, maybe, but not stupid. And I haven't had so much to drink that I can't see where this evening is headed. But even though I've never really noticed Tim Whelan before tonight, like I said, he is kind of cute and it feels nice to be with him. Plus as Cleo pointed out, I do look hot, and I think it might feel really good to kiss someone.

I guess it's time I make a major confession. Here goes: I'm pretty inexperienced with the whole guy thing. I mean, I think I have a lot of basic knowledge, but I'm kinda light in the actual hands-on experience part. Lots of girls my age have already had sex, and Cleo is going to get there pretty soon if she isn't somewhere doing it right now, and it's not like I'm ready to have sex yet, but I can count on one hand (okay, two fingers) the number of guys I've kissed, and one of those times it was during a game of truth or dare when I was in seventh grade. The other time was some real kissing (and a hand up my shirt) at a party last year, but it was with this guy who was in town visiting his cousin and he went back home to Cincinnati the next morning. Am I pathetic or what?

If Tim had asked if I wanted to go upstairs, I think I would have freaked out and said no way. But outside seems safe. There are stars outside. So we go sit on the grass with our drinks, and it doesn't take long before we're totally making out. And it feels really nice. Everything else just sort of falls away, and maybe for the first time in ages I'm not thinking of anything other than the way he smells—like apples—and the way his lips and his hands feel. I'm lying back in the grass. My head is kind of spinning. Or is it the Earth? Well, whatever it is, it's spinning fast. Really, really fast. And I'm prone to motion sickness. I get up, quickly straighten out Cleo's spandex shirt, and run over to puke in Darius's bushes.

This is not my finest hour.

Tim waits until it's clear that I am done doing what I've been doing and approaches me slowly. From a good five feet away he asks if there is anything he can get me.

"Just some water. Thanks."

You can't possibly know how sorry I feel for myself right now. Tim Whelan was kissing me. He was touching me. Me!

He hurries into the house and returns with a large plastic cup filled with lukewarm water. I drink it all in almost one gulp. My head is no longer spinning. My nausea has vanished. I'm suddenly 100 percent stone cold sober. Tim is still keeping his five-foot distance. Does he actually think I'm going to puke on him?

Just then Cleo appears. I could almost kiss her, I'm so happy to see her, although considering what I've been doing for the past few minutes, I don't think she'd appreciate that. She says that it's time for us to go home, and again I feel this rush of gratitude toward her because I know we don't really have to leave yet but she's trying to rescue me from these bushes and this party and this whole evening.

We haven't been in the car two minutes before we're both laughing pretty hard.

"So you were like totally making out with him and then you just excused yourself and hurled all over the bushes?"

"Yeah," I say. "I think he really likes me."

"Ooooh . . . Tim . . . mmmmm . . ." Cleo is making

kissing sounds. "Huuuuhhhhh." Now the sound of someone throwing up.

"Stop. You're killing me. I'm sick from laughing."

"You are such a little slut!" Cleo reaches over and kind of pushes me. "Tim Whelan! I guess he's pretty cute. He's got those really hot soccer guy legs."

I didn't notice his legs. And he was even wearing shorts! I'm light-years behind Cleo. It's always been this way with us even though I'm a full four months older than she is. Tim has hot soccer guy legs, and I didn't even think to notice.

"So," I ask her after we are done having our laugh at my expense, "anything I need to know about you and Darius?"

"No," she says. "We talked about it tonight, but I don't want to do it at some party when there are all these other people around. I want it to be . . . I don't know what I want it to be, but I don't want it to happen like that."

"Well," I say, "that makes a lot of sense to me."

We pull up in front of Cleo's house, and I'm relieved to see that the light in Jules's room and all the other lights in the house are out. I'm home safe.

six

I PROBABLY DON'T NEED TO TELL YOU that I feel absolutely awful when I wake up the next morning. For the first time in my life I know what it means to have a splitting headache. I've always had this sort of cartoon image in my mind of someone's head with all these electric currents shooting through it, splitting it into a thousand different pieces. In the cartoon the guy is holding his hands to his head, trying to keep all the pieces together, and the word balloon says something like *YEEEEOOOWWWW!!!!* That is precisely how I feel this morning. And my mouth is dry. And I smell bad.

I take some Tylenol and jump in the shower while Cleo goes downstairs to make me some coffee. I'm in a hurry. I'm due at the town hall in thirty minutes. The hot water is beating on my back, and I stare down at my feet, which I've always found to be particularly ugly, trying my best to wash away last night. I know it was funny in the car with Cleo, but today I feel pretty embarrassed. I turn the water a little hotter, almost burning my skin. How long will it take for my episode to work its way through the Twelve Oaks grapevine? Is there a speed faster than the speed of light?

When I get to the demonstration I quickly find the other members of the ASA because they're all wearing green T-shirts, as was the plan. The plan that I completely spaced on. I think it was some unconscious form of rebellion that sent me to this rally in a cherry-red shirt. I was totally against the idea that we all wear one color, but I kept quiet during the meeting because I still feel like the new kid and I don't want to make waves. We're the Atheist Student Alliance, drawn together by our common *lack* of belief. All of us wearing the same color seems counter to our mission. But this morning no one mentions my shirt. This makes me like them all a little bit more.

The Young Democrats are here, and some people from a group called Massachusetts Citizens United to Protect the Separation of Church and State, which seems like an absurdly long name for any group, and several people from a synagogue called Temple

Isaiah. I know this from the name tags that are being worn by everyone here but me. I locate the registration table, sign myself in, grab a name tag, and write SIMONE, TWELVE OAKS ASA on it. There's also fresh cider and doughnuts, but my stomach hasn't signaled its willingness to mix and mingle yet.

I find Minh, and he gives me a hug. His green T-shirt has the logo of a skateboard company on it, and he's wearing big baggy skater shorts. This is sort of a uniform for him. Minh may be an atheist, but he seems to have an almost religious devotion to skateboarding.

"Where were you last night? How come you didn't come to Rich's party?"

I just roll my eyes and shake my head, which I'm pretty sure is sign language for "You don't even want to know," and Minh lets it go. He tells me how cool the bonfire was, but of course he doesn't realize that this is like rubbing salt in my wound.

The counterdemonstration is taking place on the south side of the lawn in front of the town hall. We're standing in the shade of large red and yellow oaks that haven't yet dropped their leaves. The main demonstration is taking place across from us on the north side of the lawn under the blistering sun. You have to wonder: exactly whose side is God on here anyway?

There's a podium between the two groups—just two empty cardboard boxes one on top of the other. A rather large man steps in front of it. He is totally bald and has a full mustache. (Technically speaking, are you totally bald if you have facial hair?) People who must be members of his church surround him on all sides. Some hold signs that read YOU CAN'T CROSS OUT A CROSS. He begins to speak. No, he's not speaking, he's praying.

"Our Father, who art in heaven . . ."

You know the rest. Or maybe you don't. I'm completely surprised to learn that I actually do know the rest. Me, of all people. And I don't know how this could have happened, considering the kind of home I was raised in, yet I realize that all the words are coming to me as he is saying them.

"Give us this day our daily bread . . ."

How is this possible? By the way, I've been working pretty diligently on my vocabulary, as you know, and I think I can state with confidence that *art* is not a verb. And I have no idea what *hallowed* means.

I guess they had no takers back at the registration table because a woman approaches me with a tray of apple cider and doughnuts like this is some kind of cocktail party. Ugh. Even thinking of the word *cocktail* makes me want to hurl.

"Would you like a little refreshment, hon?" She

has gray hair that she's wearing tied back with a navy ribbon. There's a name tag on her jean jacket that says HELEN, ALL SAINTS CHURCH.

I try to be as polite as I'm able, considering my headache. "You know," I say, "I think you want to be over there." I motion to the crowd melting in the sun.

She looks puzzled. She looks at my name tag and then quickly down at her own, and a wave of understanding washes over her.

"Oh, no, dear," she says gently. "I'm in the right place. I believe the cross should be removed from our town seal. I don't think religion has any place in the public sphere."

Wow. Go, Helen. I decide to take a doughnut.

The morning passes with speeches and prayers made at the cardboard podium. Heidi speaks on behalf of the ASA and does a really great job. The rabbi from Temple Isaiah was excellent too, and he was bald with a closely trimmed beard, so I realize he's the perfect person to take my question about baldness to, but I chicken out later when he walks past me and smiles. When the mind-numbingly dull guy from the town historical society is addressing the crowd, I spot my nemesis from the Organic Oasis. This is going to be good.

I walk over to her casually. "Hi."

She looks at me and smiles. She has absolutely

no idea who I am.

"Remember me?"

She looks at me carefully. "No, I'm afraid I don't." She sticks out her hand. "I'm Laura Anderson." So now who's suddenly Ms. Hi-I'm-So-Friendly?

"I'm Simone. We met at the Organic Oasis."

It takes her a minute. "Oh, yes. That's right. The ACLU girl." She looks at my tag. "I think you need a little help with your acronym there." Now there's the lady I know and love.

"I'm not here with the ACLU today. I'm here with the Atheist Student Alliance." *Look at me! I'm a member of a club! And proud of it!*

The redness returns. And so do the whispering and the spit. I'm in complete awe of how quickly this creature can turn from smiles and sunshine into some kind of dark lord ruling over a land of fire.

"I've heard about your group," she spits, "and I intend to do something about it. My daughter is a freshman at Twelve Oaks. I'm up for a seat on the board. And when I get there you can count on your little group getting banned from campus. Good day." And again she turns around and walks away.

Well, the first thing I'm left thinking is, who the hell says "Good day" anymore? What is this, Elizabethan England? Australia? This isn't exactly how I imagined my terrible revenge. I was supposed

71

to wow her with my mastery of the issue and my wicked wit, then turn on *my* heel and leave her standing there with *her* mouth open. But today my mind and wit are as dull as that guy from the historical society. For a minute I imagine the scorecard: Evil Bitch 2, Simone 0.

I retreat back to my team of green-shirted atheists. Heidi is giving a little pep talk, thanking everyone for showing up, reminding us how important it is just to be here in numbers and how we will monitor the case, and telling us not to forget our next meeting a week from Tuesday. The doughnut is like a brick in my stomach.

"Hey, Simone. Want to go get some lunch?" It's Minh.

I don't feel like eating anything ever again and I really want to just go curl up in my bed in my stuffy attic and shut out the world, but I realize Minh is the perfect person to talk to about that telephone number, the one with the Cape Cod prefix.

We go to this new place in town called Panini. It serves—you guessed it—panini, which I believe is the plural of panino and is also just a fancy way of saying sandwich. He orders while I take a seat with a large glass of ice water.

I got to know Minh last year in chemistry when we were lab partners. We've been going to the same school for years, and I knew that he was adopted because I had seen him at different school events with his very white parents. But I never said something like "Hey, I'm adopted too. We must have a lot in common!" What kind of kid says something like that? But the truth is I made an effort to keep my distance from Minh. I didn't want to identify with him. I didn't want to talk to Minh because even though I was curious about his story I didn't want to have to tell my own. That book was closed to me. But I don't know if you've ever taken chemistry. If you have, then you will understand that during our year as lab partners Minh and I did eventually get to talking about the fact that we're both adopted because you'll end up talking about anything just so you don't have to talk about chemistry.

Minh sits down with his panino and a bottle of some kind of fancy soda that is a shocking shade of blue.

I cut to the chase. I tell him about the Rivka Situation.

Minh pushes his long hair out of his eyes and looks at me carefully. "Simone. That's so amazing. Oh my God."

"Amazing?"

"Yeah. You're so lucky. What's she like? Does she look like you? Does she have any other kids?"

I interrupt him. I have a feeling there's no end to this list of questions. The more questions he asks, the harder I have to work to prevent myself from imagining the answers.

"I have no idea. I haven't called her. I've had her phone number for a while now, and I'm not sure what to do with it."

"Are you crazy?" He looks completely baffled. "You pick up the phone and you call her. What an incredible opportunity. I would kill for a chance like this. Damn. Give me her number. I'll call her!"

Look at us sitting here. Two students at Twelve Oaks. An avid skateboarder and a newly minted member of the school newspaper. One Vietnamese boy and one olive-skinned girl. One in a green shirt and one in cherry red. If you just walked in and saw the two of us sitting here, you would have no idea that we share a past. Or what I guess I mean to say is, like atheists who share an absence of belief, we share an absence of a past. Our lives are defined by the same mystery.

"I've tried everything," he says. "The orphanage I lived in burned down years ago. My parents were never told how I got there; they only knew that I lived there since I was born. They also tell me that I seemed well fed and that I barely ever cried. I'm no real detective, but that doesn't give me much to go on."

And again, in a space of less than twenty-four hours, I feel pretty embarrassed. I've been slamming doors and crying in the dark over the chance to know something, or someone, Minh will never know. Minh can't solve his mystery, but I can begin to solve mine. Some of the answers are right in my own house, and if I want to go back farther, deeper, those answers are only ten digits away.

"Hey, Minh, I'm sorry," I start.

"Don't worry about it. Just do it. Just call her. You'll regret it if you don't."

When I return to school Monday I quickly become nostalgic for the days when I was known as the girl who's full of herself. It seems so quaint compared to the girl who was fooling around with Tim Whelan and then puked. You know what happens with rumors. By the end of the week the story has me doing much, much more with Tim than I actually was, and puking all over him instead of the bushes. I don't really know who's to blame for getting this started, but I have a hunch that Tim has something to do with it because he hasn't so much as looked in my direction all week. Forget all those things I said about him being kind of cute and smelling good and all that stuff. I hate Tim Whelan and I hate this school.

But I have bigger problems than Tim Whelan:

I can't shake my conversation with Minh.

Just call her.

Can it really be as simple as that? A telephone. A receiver pressed to my ear. A dial tone. Do ten numbers placed in a specific sequence really equal the answer to my lifetime of mystery?

Why can't my past leave me alone? Why does it keep knocking on my door, and why is this knocking getting louder and louder until I can't sleep or even think anymore?

I need the answers. I can't keep fighting them off. The knocking is getting louder, and my door is creaking open.

seven

IT WAS HALLOWEEN LAST NIGHT. Halloween is
my favorite holiday of all time. It always has been,
and not just because I'm a big fan of candy, especially
in bite-sized form. I think Halloween brings out the
very best in humanity. We open our homes and give
without expecting anything in return. It's really pretty
amazing when you think about it. What other night
do you talk to your neighbors and your neighbors'
neighbors and other people's neighbors who just
drove to your neighborhood because it seemed like a
nice place to knock on the doors of complete
strangers? What other night do you not mind when
your doorbell rings in the middle of dinner again
and again and again? On most holidays we turn
inward. We gather in our homes, we light fires, we
spend time with our loved ones. But Halloween
sends us out into the streets, into the cold, with

people we don't know, running from stranger's house to stranger's house. And in wacky costumes!

And for an atheist, Halloween is the perfect holiday. It involves spirits and the dead and generic ghosts but, from what I can tell, not the Holy Ghost. So I love Halloween. That's why I still go trick-or-treating every year. You might think people would greet a sixteen-year-old in a costume looking for candy with disdain or even hostility. But like I said, Halloween brings out the best in humanity. I was greeted only with outstretched bowls of candy and praise for my costume.

I went as Edward Scissorhands. James wore a blond wig and went as the Winona Ryder character. We looked awesome. We snagged a pretty good haul and came home and shared most of it with Jake. Then the three of us watched *Edward Scissorhands* and I went to bed early.

And then this morning I do it. I call her. My hands are shaking so much when I push the buttons that on the first try I dial a wrong number. For a minute I think this is all a hoax, that she gave me a fake number like some guy who wants you to think he likes you but really never wants to hear from you again. But when I try a second time I get a woman, just slightly out of breath, and I know immediately that I have the right number.

I'm quiet for what seems like hours but is probably only about thirty seconds. She doesn't say, "Hello? Hello? Hello?" like you usually do in that annoyed way when you answer your phone and no one is at the other end. She just stays on the line like she has all day. I can hear her catching her breath and then hear her breathing slowing down to a natural rhythm.

Finally I just say, "Hi."

Again there's a long pause.

"Simone?" she says, but it really isn't a question. She's just saying my name.

More silence.

"You know," she says, "I was just sitting in my kitchen reading my horoscope in the newspaper."

Oh, great. She's one of those crazy astrology people. I can't stand astrology people or numerology people or people who see other people's auras.

"And you should know," she says, "that I think horoscopes are complete bull and that people who believe in them should be locked away. But that being said, I read mine every day. Isn't that twisted? And today my horoscope says that someone from my past is going to make a surprise appearance."

"Wow," I say, because I'm not sure what else to say. "That's impressive."

"No. Not really. Horoscopes say crap like that almost every day. It's simple odds. They have to be right once in a while." More silence. Then the sound of a kettle boiling.

I try to picture her kitchen. Is it pale yellow? Vibrant green? Are there windows that look out into a yard or out at the ocean? Are there tall stools at a counter? A small wooden table with chairs? Are there any pots and pans hanging from the ceiling? Any plants?

And why was she out of breath? Was she racing to find the cordless phone? Was it buried between the cushions of a couch in the living room like it always is in our house?

I still don't try to picture her. I still can't.

"Did you do anything for Halloween last night?" she asks me. This throws me off. I'm not sure if she realizes how old I am, although of course she knows how old I am, but maybe she doesn't know anything about sixteen-year-olds. But then again, I did go trick-or-treating, so maybe I should say something that clearly spells out that even though I'm too old to go trick-or-treating, I did it anyway because I love Halloween.

"I was Edward Scissorhands. My friend James was Winona Ryder."

"Clever. I like that. I didn't get nearly enough trick-

or-treaters, and now I'm stuck with this huge bowl of Almond Joys and Peppermint Patties. I hate Almond Joys and Peppermint Patties. That's why I buy them— so I won't eat them all. But now I'm starting to think that maybe kids don't like them either and that's why I'm staring at a huge bowl of Almond Joys and Peppermint Patties."

"I love Almond Joys," I say. And there we have it. The first notable difference between us. "I could take or leave the Peppermint Patties."

In the next silence that follows I hear the sound of something outside far off in the distance. A car or a truck or maybe an airplane.

"Where are you?" I ask.

She understands that I don't mean in what room. Clearly she's in the kitchen. She already said so.

"Wellfleet. On the Cape." I knew it. Damn, I'm good. "It's so quiet here now. All the summer people are gone. This is my favorite time of year here, just before winter sets in and hibernation begins."

"I've never been to Cape Cod."

"How is that possible?"

"I have an uncle in Sag Harbor. We spend our beach vacations in the Hamptons."

"Big mistake."

I feel a twinge of annoyance. Who is she to judge my family or where we choose to go to the beach?

"It's really nice there. My uncle's house is just a few blocks from the water, and he has three kids all close in age to my brother and me." I say this to kind of rub her nose in my family a bit. *Look at us! We're a big, happy, fun-loving, beach-going family. And you live in your lonely little house on Cape Cod.* Or does she? Maybe her house is huge. Maybe she has a husband and a whole mess of kids running around.

"That does sound nice," she says. "I guess I'm just a snob about Cape Cod. I'm working on opening my horizons."

But I'm still thinking about who else might be in her house. Suddenly I have a desperate need to get off the phone.

"Listen, I've got to go. I'm sorry."

"Simone." There she goes again, saying my name. I think maybe she's stalling for time. She takes a deep breath and lets it out. "I'm really glad you called." And then she just lets me go.

I find my parents sitting in the living room. Dad is in his bathrobe. Mom is back from a run. Jake is still asleep in his room and will probably remain there for at least another two hours. Newspapers are everywhere (on Sundays we get both the *Boston Globe* and the *New York Times*), and I think I smell freshly squeezed oranges.

"Morning, sweets." Mom looks up from the paper and smiles. Her face is still red from the run or the cold or both. She motions for me to come and sit next to her. I oblige, and she runs her fingers through my hair. I quickly get up and go stretch out on the rug. Dad is in the armchair. Mom is on the couch. I have them both in my sight.

I reach for the comics section. I think that's where they print the horoscopes.

"I just talked to Rivka," I say.

They both quickly fold up their papers and straighten them into piles and sort of adjust themselves as if company has arrived unexpectedly. Dad goes first. "Tell us about it. How do you feel?"

"Insensate," I say. They look puzzled.

"What do you mean, honey?" Mom asks.

"I mean exactly what *insensate* means. I mean I feel nothing. I have an absence of feeling." This is of course entirely not true. I think I feel the exact opposite of insensate, but I don't know a word for feeling every emotion that exists all at once. I feel tears coming on, but this time I don't really mind.

"I think I have her voice," I say in a voice that is very quiet and shaky and not at all like my real voice.

Mom and Dad exchange looks. Then they both look at me. My mom smiles sort of sadly. "We think so too," she says.

*   *   *

Finally I have my big cry. Out in the open. Right there on the floor. With the newspapers and my mother and father as witnesses. I have to admit that it feels really good. I think the word for this is *cathartic*. I feel such overwhelming relief. My head is clearing, and at the same time it's spinning with questions. I've kept them locked out for so long, and now the window has been thrown open and they are swarming in. There are so many questions that I hardly know where to begin. But while I was listening to the sound of Rivka's voice and of her home and of her life in the background I realized that my first questions aren't for Rivka. They're for Mom and Dad. They tell me they have some answers whenever I'm ready. I'm grateful to them for leaving it at that and understanding that the Big Cry pretty much tapped me out for at least today, probably for longer.

Dad then does what Dad does best. He feeds me. He makes raspberry-banana pancakes, turkey sausages, and some scrambled eggs I leave untouched. I drink two huge glasses of orange juice and more coffee than I should. Jake finally stumbles out of his room (shirtless, of course), eats about twice what I did, and then polishes off my eggs. I take a close look at him, searching for signs of my little brother. Everything about him is changing. He sleeps forever. His appetite knows no bounds. His voice is deeper than Dad's. And I think I've already mentioned his budding physique. Jake is in the middle of a spectacular transformation, and the signs of it are everywhere you turn. But here I am, sitting across from Jake while rapid and irreversible changes are happening to me, and if you took a closer look, you still wouldn't be able to see anything at all.

In the afternoon I go apple picking with my family. I was supposed to see a movie with Cleo and Ivy, but when my dad suggests that we go apple picking, it just seems like the perfect way to spend the day. And it was. I don't mean to make it sound sickeningly sweet, like look at this perfect family laughing and smiling and filling bushels with bright red apples and then piling the bushels into the back of their Subaru wagon and heading home, leaving whirling trails of brightly colored leaves on the country road behind them. But that's pretty much how it was. I'm just happy to be with my family today. They make me laugh, and they also make me proud, and they make me feel safe. I think maybe I give Jake one too many completely uncalled-for squeezes around the neck, because he finally just looks at me and says, "What's with you today, you freak?"

And I go to bed in my attic, under my fading glow-in-the-dark stars, with my fingers still stinging from the November cold and my eyes still stinging from this morning's Big Cry, and I sleep a sleep without dreaming.

eight

DID I MENTION that Amy Flannigan is also on staff at the *Oaks Gazette*? This makes it all but impossible ever to have a conversation with Zack Meyers alone. I know everyone says that they're just best friends, but if that's true, you'd think she could spread the wealth a little bit and let Zack talk to another member of the female species unsupervised. But no. When Zack and I are finally assigned to the same story, we make a plan to meet at the *Gazette* office after school. And guess who's hanging out with him when I arrive? You got it.

It's a pretty unusual assignment for the *Gazette* and for me too. I'm writing a story about my mother. I just realized how that sounds. Let me clarify: I'm writing a story about my mother, not about Rivka. The idea came up at a staff meeting, and Marcel, the editor, suggested that we do a profile on the lawyer who is bringing the town seal case. He didn't know that she's my mother. You can probably imagine how fast my heart raced when Zack interrupted and said, "The lawyer's name is Elsie Turner, and she's Simone's mom."

Everyone agreed that it would be a pretty cool piece for the paper, especially if I wrote it. Then Zack volunteered to take the pictures.

We're meeting today so that he can go over a draft of my story and brainstorm some ideas of how to take an interesting companion photograph.

We stand around talking for a little bit, all three of us. But when I dig my draft out of my backpack and hand it to Zack, he takes a seat at one of the tables and says goodbye to Amy. She's dismissed. Zack puts his elbows on the table, holds his head in both hands, and starts reading my article. He's gripping a red pen. I'm biting my cuticles. I think I may be sweating, and I pray to the God whom I forsake that my deodorant does what the label guarantees it will do for its full twelve hours of long-lasting protection.

He looks up. "This is pretty good."

Let me translate for you. What Zack just said is: *This is the worst piece of crap I've ever read. You are an illiterate moron.*

"Thanks," I say lamely.

"I mean it's pretty good."

"Thanks," I say again. *Oh, Jesus.*

"Well, what I mean to say is, I think you can do better." *Ouch.*

"Yeah? How so?"

"Well . . . you can go deeper than just the facts of this case and how it came to the ACLU and why your mom decided to take it." He pauses. "Look, I love your writing."

Did he just say he loved me? No. Get a grip. He said he loved my writing.

"But this piece is a little flat, which is surprising considering your access and your relationship to the subject. Or maybe that's the problem. . . . I think you need to try to forget that she's your mom when you do the interview."

I guess maybe he's right. I did throw this together pretty quickly based on a series of short conversations I've had with Mom over the past few days. I guess I thought I could kind of sit back and let the whole mother-daughter aspect of it work on its own. Clearly I was wrong. I have delivered a piece of crap. A "little flat" piece of crap.

Zack readjusts his glasses and kind of tugs at his earring. "Start with what inspires her. Not just about this case. Maybe you should start by asking her about her first big case as a young lawyer and what she learned from that experience. Make this more of a personal journey for her."

And that is how Zack Meyers, without knowing it, and without knowing nearly anything about me or my family, became responsible for my finally learning how Rivka came into my parents' lives, and how I then came into theirs.

His name was Mordechai Levin. But everyone just called him the Rebbe. He lived in a suburb south of Boston with his wife and seven children. That's right. I said seven. Apparently Hasidic Jews don't believe in birth control, but beyond that, they believe that God commands them to have tons of kids. God said, "Be fruitful and multiply." And they do because that's what God said. So I guess having sex is a way of serving God. (Maybe Cleo should have tried out this excuse on Jules when Jules found out that she and Darius are having sex. More on that later.) Anyway, Mordechai was the spiritual leader of this small but densely packed Hasidic community south of Boston. Hasidic Judaism, I've learned, because I'd never heard of it before, is a type of ultra-Orthodox Judaism. You can picture Orthodox Jews, right? All I know is that the men have big beards, heavy dark clothes, and funny hats, and the women have long skirts and bad hair. (The hair is actually a wig! *That* I didn't know.) So Mordechai was the spiritual leader of this community, and that's why they called him the Rebbe.

Every Friday night and then again on Saturday morning all these Hasids would gather in the Rebbe's rather large home and worship and pray and sometimes read from the Torah (which is what they call the first five books of the Old Testament) and listen to the Rebbe's sermons. And basically, this started to piss off some of the Rebbe's neighbors. Because like I said, the Rebbe lived in this suburb south of Boston. And when I said that the community was densely packed with Hasidic Jews, I meant that there were a lot more Hasidic Jews living there than there are in most other communities, like mine for instance, but I didn't mean that there were *only* Hasidic Jews living there. In this suburb there were also tons of Irish Catholics and all sorts of other Christians and non-believing people like me. On the Rebbe's street there was a businessman who commuted to the city and his schoolteacher wife, a family who owned a gardening shop, and a woman who worked out of her house selling computer software over the telephone. None of these people took kindly to the Friday night and Saturday morning parades of Hasids marching up and down their street on their way to the Rebbe's house. So what did they do? They called the town zoning commission and ratted out the Rebbe. Because according to the zoning laws, it was forbidden to operate any kind of business, which includes a house of worship, on a residential street. And what did the Rebbe do when his disgruntled neighbors ratted him out? He called the ACLU. And that is how Mom comes into this story.

This might seem strange given what you know about Mom and her devout atheism and her fight to get the cross removed from our town seal, but she didn't hesitate in taking the Rebbe's case. The ACLU, she will tell you, exists to defend the freedom and liberty of everyone. That includes protecting not only an individual's freedom from religion but also an individual's freedom of religion. In other words, the government shouldn't force you into a religion like they do when they put a cross on your town seal, but they also shouldn't prevent you from being able to practice whatever religion you choose. Mom took the case because if the Hasids of this little suburb were not allowed to worship in the Rebbe's house, then they would have been unable to worship at all. Hasidic Jews can't travel on the Sabbath. They can't drive cars or take buses or taxis. They gathered at the Rebbe's house because there was nowhere else for them to worship within walking distance of where they all lived.

When Mom first met the Rebbe, she disliked him immediately.

His wife, Hannah, led Mom into his study for their first meeting about the case. Hannah knocked gently on his door, opened it slowly, and said, "The lawyer from the ACLU is here." My mother, twenty-eight years old and sporting a new leather briefcase, entered his poorly lit study.

He looked up from his papers and at my mother with a puzzled expression. Mordechai's beard was thick and black, without a trace of gray even though he was not a particularly young man and had a house filled with seven children. He leaned back. He tugged at his beard.

"They sent a woman," he said.

"I'm not sure who you think 'they' are, Mr. Levin," Mom said. "But I am the one who decided to take your case. We spoke on the phone. Remember?"

"Yes, I remember. But I believed that you were the receptionist or perhaps the legal secretary."

My mother fought off the urge to use a word from her deep reserves of profanity. "Well, I'm not, Mr. Levin. I'm your lawyer."

He looked at her for a long time and then motioned to the chair facing his desk. "Please have a seat. And please, it's Rabbi Levin."

Over the six months that they worked together, the Rebbe and my mother came to have a civil but not friendly relationship. On the other hand, Mom and Hannah, in those brief moments before Hannah would deliver Mom to Mordechai's study, discovered that they shared more in common than you would imagine. Hannah had an extremely analytical mind that was greatly underused in her role as the Rebbetzen, which is what they call the Rebbe's wife. Not only was Hannah a homemaker and the primary caregiver for her brood of seven, but as the Rebbetzen she was expected to play hostess and advisor and confidante to all of the women in the community, and this was not a role that she particularly enjoyed. So Hannah looked forward to Mom's visits because it gave her a chance to talk about things that she didn't generally have the opportunity to talk about with anyone else.

Mom also started to get to know some of the children in the Levin house. There was the eldest, a quiet and beautiful girl about sixteen years old with long straight dark hair and almond eyes. Then there were three boys, each separated by just one year, who were almost indistinguishable to Mom but who were equally loud and sweet and funny. Then there were two younger girls, neither as beautiful as their older sister, and a baby who never seemed to be out of Hannah's arms.

*   *   *

One afternoon, about four months after Mom had started regularly visiting the Levin house, she was surprised to find the eldest daughter at the front door.

"Can we take a walk?" she asked my mother.

Mom didn't quite know what to say to this girl. So she asked for Hannah.

"She's not here this afternoon. She has an appointment. Please. I really need to talk to you."

Mom peeked behind her into the house and could see Mordechai's closed study door at the end of the hallway.

"Let me just—"

"No," the girl interrupted. "Please. I don't want him to know."

So Mom went for a walk with this girl because she saw something desperate in her eyes, and at twenty-eight she didn't feel too far away from her own years of teenage isolation and the times that she'd wished there were someone she could talk to.

And on this walk through the neighborhood of this little suburb south of Boston, while paused under a large oak with almost no leaves left on it (because like it is here now, it was November then), Mordechai and Hannah Levin's eldest child, their daughter Rivka, told my mother that she was pregnant.

nine

MOM WON HER CASE. It was her first big victory as a young lawyer; it got a lot of press and put her on the map in the legal community, and it helped shape her views on religion and freedom. This is what made it into my article for the *Oaks Gazette*. It made for a great story, and Zack took a really cool picture with Mom in front of a church holding a sword and a shield, which, in case you don't get Zack's brilliance, showed her as both an aggressor against and a protector of religion. That's what I wrote about, even though for Mom, everything about her first big case was eclipsed by this young girl and her sidewalk confession made on that November afternoon.

Rivka didn't know who else to turn to, and she figured that my mother, this liberal lawyer from the city, could help her find a place to get an abortion.

Of course, Mom was a firm believer in a woman's

right to choose, but she had never come face to face with this belief. And here was Rivka's face, not the face of a woman but that of a girl—young, frightened, and confused. Before this moment, choice was an abstract concept to Mom. It was an idea to believe in. It was something to fight for. But now here it stood, right in front of her, asking for help, asking what to do, asking that Mom be the lawyer, judge, and jury.

She said she would do whatever she could to get Rivka through this, but that Rivka needed to talk to her parents first. At this suggestion Rivka sat down, right there in the middle of the sidewalk under the oak tree, and wept. She said her parents would disown her; she said that she would bring shame upon the Rebbe's house. She said it would be the end of her life. Mom had spent enough time by now with Mordechai to know that Rivka was probably right about how he would react, but Mom had also caught glimpses of a Hannah who might be able to see things differently.

Mom was right. Hannah, before being a Hasidic Jew, before being the Rebbetzen, before being anything else, was a mother who loved her daughter. She didn't want Rivka, at the age of sixteen, to have a baby. But she also didn't want Rivka to have an abortion.

Hannah asked Mom to help them find a home for the baby, a good home with a good family. Her contact with the world beyond the Hasids in their little community was limited. She didn't know where to go or who to call or what to do.

Hannah wanted this done quietly. No one was to know, especially not the Rebbe. It was to their advantage that he never took a careful look at his daughter and that the Hasidic uniform of long skirts and ill-fitting tops was naturally forgiving to someone in Rivka's condition. She would need only a few larger, baggier outfits in the final months. As it turned out, Rivka was already four and a half months pregnant and was hardly showing. Hannah fully expected that Rivka would carry this baby neatly and close to her slender frame, just as Hannah had done with all seven of her pregnancies.

On some days the dual role Mom played in the Levin house would be too much for her. She would come home to the little apartment she shared with her boyfriend, Vince Bloom, only twenty-five and a student at the art institute, exhausted, teary, depressed, and filled with anxiety. Her sleeplessness kept him up at night. They talked of almost nothing else.

One night, about five weeks after Rivka's sidewalk

confession, Mom got off the train, briefcase in hand, and walked up the snow-covered cobblestone street in Beacon Hill where she and Vince lived. She could see into the second-floor window of their apartment. The living room was illuminated by an unusual light, soft and full of movement, as if there were a fire in the fireplace she always wished they had. She left her boots in the entryway and unlocked the front door. Vince was sitting on the couch clutching a bouquet of white tulips. The flames from hundreds of tiny votive candles flickered everywhere.

"What's going on in here?" was all my mother could say, and it occurred to her right then that she sounded just like her own mother did when she discovered her children doing something they shouldn't.

"Come here," Vince said, and patted the couch next to him. He took away her briefcase and took my mother's hands. He put the tulips down on the coffee table. Their stems had been crushed by his nervous grip.

"I know this sounds crazy, Elsie, but I think we should do this. I think we should take this baby. We may be young and stupid and have absolutely no experience with babies, but nobody knows what they're doing when they first have a baby, and I think we'll be just as good at not knowing what we're doing as anybody else. And," my father said, "I want you to marry me."

During all of their late-night conversations about Rivka and Hannah and Mordechai they had never discussed the possibility that they adopt Rivka's baby. And it wasn't until she saw Vince sitting there in the candlelight with the crushed tulips, the ink from his drawing class still under his fingernails, that Mom was able to admit that in her secret heart she had imagined them taking and raising this child. Even though neither of them was a believer in fate or destiny or God, they agreed that this was simply what was meant to be. It was decided then and there. They drank a very expensive bottle of wine and looked around their tiny apartment and wondered where they would fit all of the things that go along with having a baby.

They were married three days later at city hall and would have done it even sooner if it weren't for the three days it takes to get a marriage license in the state of Massachusetts.

So there you have it. That's pretty much how I got here. Did you catch the part where my parents weren't even married? For some reason, this rocks my world more than almost anything else. It's sort of the reverse of those stories you hear about people who get married because they find out that, whoops, we're having a baby, we'd better hurry up and get married. No. My parents thought, *Wow, there's this baby out there and we really want her, so quick, let's get married and make ourselves look respectable so we can adopt her.* And I suddenly feel this intimacy with them that is not at all strange because I was there with them that night almost seventeen years ago when they decided to get married.

For so long I've been so good at keeping information out, and now I've just opened up the floodgates and let all this stuff in, and I can't seem to rid my thoughts of Rivka and Mordechai and Hannah and all those other nameless Levin kids. These people aren't even real to me, yet they won't leave me alone, and it's hard for me to find moments when they aren't with me, tapping on my shoulder or tugging on my sleeve. And did I mention that my parents think we should invite Rivka for Thanksgiving?

Talking to Cleo has always been a good way to clear my head, but these days lunchtime at school is about the only time I get to talk to her about the sex that she and Darius aren't having because Jules won't let her leave the house or even talk on the phone. Just to back up for a minute: Cleo and Darius finally started having sex. Their first time was at Darius's house when his parents were away for yet another weekend and just for a change he wasn't having a party. Since that first time it seems like they'll do it anywhere there's a horizontal surface and a door that closes, although sometimes they've gone at it without one or the other. Usually they just go to Cleo's house after school. Sure enough, one day last week Jules came home early with an upset stomach that probably wasn't helped by the scene she discovered in Cleo's bedroom. You already know how I feel about the prospect of catching my parents in the act, so when I try to put myself in Jules's position I really feel for her. And God knows I spend enough time trying to put myself in Cleo's position. Wait. That sounds a lot dirtier than I intended it to. What I mean to say is, for me, having sex seems like something I will do one day, on another planet, in a galaxy far, far away. So for now I have only Cleo's experience to live through.

When I find Cleo in the cafeteria she's sitting with James and they're both pouting. Apparently I'm not the only one with Thanksgiving problems. (Again, I'd like to give a shout out to Halloween and its complete lack of complication.) Cleo is still furious about having to go to Arizona, but she can't complain anymore because she gave up the moral high ground with Jules the minute Jules threw open the door to Cleo's bedroom. James was thinking about visiting Patrick in New York, but Patrick hasn't thought enough about James to return any of his last three phone calls. When I tell them that my parents want to invite Rivka to our house for Thanksgiving, James and Cleo do what good friends do and quickly make it seem as if my Rivka problem trumps their Arizona and Patrick problems, but I know that there's no winner here. Now the three of us are pouting when the bell for fifth period rings.

In history class I stare out the window. It's a pretty nasty day, and I think it fairly well mimics my mood. I wish I were Cleo, not because of her boobs or because of the sex, although I'll admit that I'm curious about what it would feel like to have either. I just wish I could go three thousand miles away for Thanksgiving, where it's hot and dry and flat and different in every way from what it's like right here. Maybe we could switch places. It's a brilliant plan. Rivka wouldn't even have to know. And it's been so long since Cleo has seen Edward, he might not notice either.

I have a *Gazette* meeting after school. Even there I can't seem to pay attention. I'm sleepwalking through my life. During the meeting I further examine what I have come to think of as the Zack and Amy Conundrum. Zack and Amy's relationship, like the existence of God, defies everything I know about logic. I try to apply some simple formulaic thinking: if Z and A are always together and if A keeps Z from ever talking to another girl, then Z and A *must* be more than friends. Right? At the very least A is in love with Z. But I can't seem to crack this question: is Z in love with A?

I try this out on James, who is giving me a lift home from school. He doesn't even know about my crush. I'm slower than most of my friends to share this kind of information, because unlike Cleo, it doesn't usually end up with me getting the guy.

"Is he the one with the camouflage high-tops and Flash Gordon earring?"

"Flash Gordon? I guess I thought of it as a Harry Potter earring, but yes."

"Well, whatever it is, it has to go."

"You're missing the point."

"Ah, yes . . . the are-they-or-aren't-they question. Well, you've come to the right place. I am the resident expert on sublimated sexuality."

James clears his throat, straightens a nonexistent tie, and launches into a mock lecture about people who are clearly in love but for one reason or another never act on their sexual feelings and instead develop all the trappings of a relationship without consummating it.

"Like me and Graham," James says, referring to this guy in our class he's always had a crush on and who has never given him the time of day, "except without the whole developing-the-trappings-of-a-relationship thing."

"Or even the acknowledging-the-other-person's-existence thing."

James laughs. "Flash Gordon is awfully cute, Simone. But you don't want to get tangled up with that."

"Are you saying that a guy and a girl can't ever be best friends?"

"If they're just best friends, then why does she give you the evil eye whenever you go near him? Come on. Haven't you ever seen any teen movies? It always ends with the best friends realizing they're in love. Then the cheesy pop melody kicks in, and the camera does a complete rotation around them while they share their first kiss using way too much tongue."

"This is depressing."

"This is reality."

This is what I love about James. He never tells you what you want to hear just because that's what you want to hear.

My mother, on the other hand, tells me when I get home that we have to make a decision about Rivka and Thanksgiving and she's leaving that decision up to me. This is what she thinks I want to hear, that it's my decision, like I really have a choice in the matter. It's funny how parents do that. They're tremendously skilled at making you think you're in control when really they're just hovering somewhere high above you like master puppeteers, tugging at all of your strings. Right hand up. Left hand down. Head from side to side. Call Rivka. Invite her for Thanksgiving.

But I'm older now. I'm wiser. This time I see right through her. "Obviously your mind is made up about this, so why don't *you* invite her and stop pretending that I have anything to do with this decision?"

"No, Simone, this is really up to you," says Mom.

"That is such a lie! If this were really up to me, we wouldn't even be having this conversation. If this were really up to me, you'd just say hi and let me go up to my room and not make me come sit here on the couch and listen to another one of your lectures."

Where's Dad? Why did he leave me here alone, defenseless against Mom? I feel like one of those baby animals on a nature program, trying to graze peacefully in a field while a puma is circling me behind the tall grass.

"What I mean to say, Simone, is that it's up to you to offer this invitation. I'm not going to do this for you. I think it's the right thing to do. She's reached out to you; now it's your turn. But if you don't want to do it, I'm not going to force you, and I'm not going to make the call for you."

I sit there for a long time after Mom has left the room, staring at the floor. Then I go up to my room, shut the door, and pick up the phone.

ten

OUR HOUSE SMELLS LIKE CINNAMON. I've never been a big fan of cinnamon, but Dad keeps telling me I won't taste it. Hard to imagine how this is possible when its smell is overpowering every other ingredient in the kitchen. Rivka is due to arrive in about an hour. I'm hiding out in the attic.

So of course I called Rivka and invited her for Thanksgiving, and obviously she accepted or else I wouldn't be up here. Our conversation didn't go much beyond this invitation, although I did ask if there was anyone she wanted to bring with her, and she said that she would be coming alone. Scratch the image of a house filled with kids. Put a question mark next to the husband.

My first meeting with Rivka was starting to have a feeling of inevitability about it, so I figured why not have it at my house on my turf? It's strange, but I just somehow know that this is where things have to go, so I'm going along with it. It's like a story is being written, and it requires that the character of Simone and the character of Rivka finally meet face to face. I can't do anything about it, and I don't really want to do anything about it anymore. I want to see her face.

When I was little I never played with dolls. I never had baby dolls with little changeable outfits. I never had a doll who closed her eyes when you tilted her head back, or said "mama," or, like Cleo's doll, peed when you fed her a bottle of water. (I always thought that was kind of gross.) And I never, ever played with Barbie dolls because in my house Barbie was pretty much the devil incarnate. But I did have this one soft toy that I never would have called a doll, though it had yarn for hair and a flat, soft face with painted-on features. I had her for years. She went through the wash so many times that eventually her features faded to nothing. This is what Rivka has become to me. She's not a mongoose from a famous children's story. She's not a place. She's a person with a blank space where a face would be. While some things are becoming clearer and some blanks are being filled in, I still can't imagine her face. And in about an hour or so I won't have to.

*   *   *

Jake comes up to the attic to ask if he can borrow my headphones.

"Why? What's wrong with yours?"

"They're broken."

"That makes sense."

"Huh?"

"Your head seems to get bigger and bigger every day now that you're this supercool high school jock. These things aren't made of elastic, Jake." I toss him my headphones.

He laughs and says, "Ha ha, very funny," and tells me to shut up, but he looks a little hurt. I can't help it. Everything just seems so easy for Jake. He moved effortlessly from adorable little boy to hot freshman guy without his nose and Adam's apple growing at twice the rate as the rest of him. He's a great athlete. Teachers love him. He has tons of friends. I've heard there are several junior and even senior girls with crushes on him. And he has only one mother and one father, both downstairs in the kitchen cooking a Thanksgiving dinner with too much cinnamon in it.

"Simone, are you okay with this today?"

To top it all off, he's unbelievably sweet.

"I guess so."

"Well, that's good, because I'm kind of freaking out."

This catches me off guard. I didn't ever stop to

think about what effect all this might be having on Jake. "Why?"

"I don't know."

It was a big enough step for Jake to come up here and admit that the Rivka Situation is bothering him; I can't expect him to actually articulate *why* it's bothering him. I didn't even need to ask him why, because it makes perfect sense to me. This must disrupt Jake's world and his sense of our family.

Jake sits down in the armchair. "I don't want her here. I wish she would just go away, and I don't really understand why Mom and Dad have been making such a big deal about this."

The boy has a point. I can't figure this out either. They still haven't given me a reasonable explanation. Why are they forcing this on me? Why now?

Jake looks so unhappy. "You know Mom and Dad," I say. "This is just part of their whole approach to life. They need to talk about everything. They need to process everything. They want everything out in the open. It's one of the hazards of having hippie do-gooders for parents."

"Yeah, well, whatever. I think their timing sucks. I just want to have my Thanksgiving in peace, and now it's going to be all weird."

"No, it won't, Jake. It'll be just another family Thanksgiving. I mean, what's weird about having a

Thanksgiving turkey with Mom and Dad and you and me and some lady who gave birth to me sixteen and a half years ago and hasn't seen me since?"

"Oh, yeah. You're right. Nothing at all."

Jake sinks deeper into the chair and leans his head back, and I can see the tension leave his body. I guess he just needed to know that I'm still able to joke about this, that I'm still the sister he knows and loves. We stay up in my attic together until we hear the doorbell ring.

It's a false alarm. It's just Jules. She's come to join us for Thanksgiving and a front-row seat to the Simone freak show. Cleo left for Arizona last night, and I've already talked to her twice. She said that the little girl whose name she can't remember (Carly) is fat and that she thinks the little boy (Craig) has Tourette's syndrome because he constantly blurts out "penis" for no apparent reason. They're having some kind of southwestern Thanksgiving meal involving chipotle chiles and cilantro that Cleo says her "mommy" has spent days preparing. She thinks it's funny to call Edward's wife her "mommy," and she's pretty sure that Edward and the wife don't find it so funny, which makes Cleo think it's even funnier. She says that the pool has too much chlorine in it and she misses Darius. This I don't really understand. Well, I do understand that too much chlorine can be really unpleasant, but I don't understand Cleo missing Darius. Does she miss Darius or does she miss having sex with Darius? Because to me, the sex seems to be the cornerstone of their relationship.

During our second conversation of the day, when for the third time she mentioned how much she missed Darius, I just asked her, "Are you in love with him?"

Cleo laughed. "Honestly, Simone, grow up."

"Screw you, Cleo."

"Come on. I didn't mean it like that. I just mean that nobody cares about love or being in love anymore."

"What, you mean love went out along with the grunge look?"

"No, I mean it's just not something I spend time worrying about. I just like to be with him and I don't want him to be with anyone else, and that's all I know for now."

Cleo. She's four months younger than me and still seems like my older, wiser sister. I hung up the phone feeling annoyed and also sort of foolish. Yes, she did tell me to grow up, and that accounts at least in part for my feeling annoyed and foolish, but also no one bothered to tell me that love is out, and I walk around still believing in it or searching for it or at the very least trying to make some sense of it.

When I see Jules down in the kitchen she asks, "Have you heard from Cleo?"

"Yeah. Haven't you?"

"Of course. She's having a good time, isn't she?"

"I guess."

Cleo is never all that forthcoming with Jules, even in the best of circumstances, so I'm pretty sure Jules is trying to pump me for information, but this is *my* day for weird family stuff. I don't have time for anyone else's drama.

Rivka was due five minutes ago. Maybe she got cold feet. Maybe she decided to keep driving north and is headed toward New Hampshire or Canada or somewhere beyond the Arctic Circle.

I can hear the sound of a clock ticking, but I notice that the only clock in the room is digital, so I must be losing my mind. Everyone is doing his or her best to pretend that this is just another Thanksgiving meal, just some family and friends hanging out in the kitchen with nothing out of the ordinary about to happen.

The doorbell rings.

Everyone freezes and stares at me. We didn't plan this out. We didn't decide who was going to greet her at the door, take her coat, ask her if she wants a drink.

Without saying anything, I get up. The sound my stool makes as it drags along the kitchen floor could shatter glass. Mom grabs my arm.

"Do you want me to go?"

I put my hand over hers. "No, Mom, it's okay. I've got it."

Let me back up just a minute here to say that with everything that's been going on and everything I've learned and all the mysteries and surprises and the other things that I can't even begin to come to terms with, I haven't dwelled at all on the fact that Rivka is a Hasidic Jew. You'd think that this would be at the top of my list of hard things to deal with, and I don't in any way mean to sound xenophobic or anything, but it's pretty strange, especially considering my outlook on God and religion. I guess right now everything seems so strange to me that it's hard to separate out the *really* strange from the just plain strange. So I made a note of this fact, Rivka—Hasidic Jew—and then kind of placed it in my file of information without examining it too carefully.

But as I reach for the door handle, I access the file with the image of a woman in a long dark skirt, a boxy blouse, and a wig.

I open the door to find a woman with her own short, dark straight hair wearing blue jeans, brown suede boots, an orange V-neck sweater, and a killer shade of lipstick. She's young and she's beautiful. As for her age, this I could easily have figured out if I'd bothered to stop and think. She was sixteen on that November afternoon seventeen years ago. So right now, on this Thanksgiving Day, Rivka is only thirty-three. As for her beauty, I have this immediate reaction that I'm embarrassed to admit to, but here goes anyway. I think: *Wow, maybe there's still hope for me.*

I meet her eyes, her almond eyes, and hers meet mine, and we stand there for a moment. She takes a step back. And another one. She sits down on the bench on our porch and says, "I don't know about you, but I could use some air."

She already needs air and she hasn't even set foot in our cinnamon-scented house. But I've been in here all day and I actually could use some air because I feel like I might pass out, so I close the front door behind me and sit in an old wooden rocker. I'm not quite facing her, but I'm positioned in such a way that I can get a good look at her without seeming like I'm staring her down.

"Thanks for inviting me," she says. "I know this must be strange for you. It sure as hell is strange for me."

I sneak a quick look, and the thing is, she looks

completely and immediately familiar to me. I can't pick out anything unusual or surprising in her face. It's as if I've looked at her face every day of my life, and I don't say this as a way of telling you that it's like looking into a mirror, because it's not, I'm different. But I don't know how else to describe it—her face is just *familiar* to me.

Her brown boots (I'd love a pair just like them) and her jeans and orange V-neck sweater, unlike her face, catch me by surprise.

"I thought you were Hasidic."

I would never in a million years have imagined that these would be the first words I would speak to my birth mother face to face. But there you have it.

"And I thought you had blue eyes." She looks down and shakes her head as if she wishes she could take that back. "I mean, that's what I remember about you from the day you were born. I thought you had blue eyes, and I couldn't understand how that could be."

I don't know what to say, so I just sit there slowly rocking in the rocking chair.

"I guess all babies' eyes look kind of blue at birth and the true color doesn't develop until months later, and of course I wasn't around months later to see that your eyes aren't blue at all. Your eyes are brown. I don't think there's ever been a blue eye in my family, and God knows, with all of the kids and kids' kids, we certainly have given the gene pool enough of an opportunity to cough one up. Oh, Jesus. I'm rambling, aren't I? I do that when I'm nervous. I'm making a total ass out of myself."

"No, you're not. It's okay." Look at me, acting like the grown-up, trying to make this easier on *her*, smoothing things over for *her*. I have a sudden impulse to break the silence that has come over us with a scream that would echo on my front porch and across the snow-covered lawns down my street: *What about me?* But of course I don't. I sit here quietly and rock.

"About the Hasidic thing," she says. "That isn't who I am anymore. You don't really know who I was, so maybe that doesn't mean much to you, but anyway, it's not who I am anymore."

"You aren't Jewish?"

"I didn't say that. Look, this is complicated. I'd love to talk about it with you sometime, but it's going to take a longer conversation than we can have right now, and anyway, I want to know about you. Tell me something about you."

"I'm hungry," I say, and stand up and invite Rivka into my home.

eleven

DINNER WAS DELIGHTFUL. We stuffed ourselves. We talked about how thankful we are. We laughed uproariously. Then we gathered around the piano and linked arms and sang show tunes. Okay, none of that is true. Well, maybe *Dad* stuffed himself, but we don't even have a piano. Dinner was strange. Horror-movie strange. Foreboding tinkly music strange. If it *had* been a horror movie, something would have burst through the walls and everyone would have screamed and the table would have been kicked over, and I found myself thinking that it would have been a relief if something, anything, had burst through the walls and put an end to the awkward silences.

Good old Jules tried her best to fill those silences with tales from her last few terrible dates, which included one with a guy who had a home gym but not one book anywhere in the entire house. Literally.

Or *illiterately*. (That was Jules's stupid joke, not mine, and Rivka didn't laugh, so at least I know she has a good sense of humor.) I kept looking at the six of us around the table trying to figure where Rivka fit in. She seemed trapped somewhere between the adults and the children. Obviously Rivka is an adult. She's thirty-three. But she isn't as old as Mom and Dad and Jules, and the last time Mom and Dad saw her she was exactly my age, so I think they must in some way still view her as this helpless young girl, and this made the dinner-table dynamic kind of strange. There's that word again: *strange*. I'm aware that I've used this word way too many times. I know plenty of synonyms for *strange: perplexing, astonishing, eccentric*. Even though these are perfectly good words in their own right, none of them applies to this day or to my life lately as well as the word *strange* does, so that is why I keep using it again and again and again.

We move into the living room for dessert, and this change helps ease some of the tension. I think about how in almost every other house across the nation today, this is the moment when people loosen their belts or undo the top buttons of their pants. But for us, at this moment, when we move from the hard, straight-backed dining room chairs to the comfortable couches in the living room, we all seem to loosen something inside us.

Jules takes a bite of the pie she brought and asks, "So, Rivka, what do you do?"

This is the first real question anyone has asked her. That's probably why Mom and Dad invited Jules. They know her tendency to talk a lot and ask a lot of questions, and I guess they figured she would probably step up if I sat there like the mute I've been all afternoon.

"I'm a photographer."

A photographer. Like Zack Meyers. I've never spent much time messing around with a camera, but maybe I should. Maybe I could be a photographer.

"What do you photograph?" I ask her. "Or is it what's your subject? Or what do you shoot? What's the right way to ask someone who takes pictures what they like to take pictures of?"

Rivka smiles. "Any of those will do."

She folds one leg underneath her. I look down at my lap. I'm sitting in the exact same position.

"I mostly photograph landscapes. I live on Cape Cod, so that includes a lot of beaches and sand dunes and grass. One of the reasons I live there is because of the light. The Cape has the most amazing light."

"And you make enough money doing that, taking pictures of the beach?" This comes out a little harsher than I intended. I don't even know who I sound like. Neither of my parents would ever phrase a question like that.

"Mountains of money," she says, deadpan. "I'm loaded."

"Really?"

"Not at all. But I do have my work in several galleries on the Cape, and it does sell from time to time, mostly to rich tourists. I also shoot family pictures, portraits; I've done a few weddings. Last month this couple in Truro hired me to take photographs of their schnauzers."

Jake has been lying on the floor. He props himself up on one elbow. "Did they dress them up in little outfits? I hate people who dress up their dogs."

"No. They were as naked as the day they were born."

"So you shoot doggie porno?" I ask.

Rivka laughs. "Yes, but only very tasteful doggie porno."

Dad disappears out of the room and comes back with two sets of Scrabble. Leave it to Dad to have an extra set on hand. He's such a Scrabble freak. My family always plays on Thanksgiving, and since we have six people Dad suggests that we do a sort of round robin where there are two games of three people each and then the winners play each other in a final face-off. He's the only one excited by this idea: Dad is highly competitive. None of us agrees to the final round, so two winners there will be. Dad pouts as he takes his seat at the board with Mom and Jake. Jules and Rivka and I set up next to them. Despite Jules's earlier joke about illiteracy, she does a miserable job against Rivka and me, who are neck and neck through the whole game until I dump my final letters and win by going out on the three-letter word *kin*.

I'm showing Rivka my attic. I feel a little like I did when I was younger and used to have friends over and we'd go barricade ourselves in my room and whisper about things we didn't want the grown-ups to hear. But of course Rivka is a grown-up and I'm not a little kid anymore. And we don't have to whisper because now I live in the attic.

"This is a real oasis up here, isn't it?" she asks me.

I nod.

"I would have killed for a space like this when I was your age. I shared my room with my younger sisters, and our house was always filled with people. I never had anywhere to be by myself when I was growing up."

"And yet you still found the time and space to get pregnant. Amazing."

She doesn't stare at me or look hurt or startled or anything.

"Yes, well, I guess you wouldn't be surprised to

know that it didn't happen in my little room in my crowded house."

"How did it happen?" This is the question that's been on my mind all through dinner and dessert and Scrabble. While I've been visited throughout my life by thoughts and images of Rivka, I've never stopped to think about *him*. But now that she's before me and I can finally see her and study her and no longer have to imagine her, the mathematical part of me suddenly needs to fill in the other properties. I need the second half of the equation.

"I take it you don't really mean *how*?"

"No, I'm pretty up to speed on how babies are made. I mean *who*. Who was he?"

She takes a deep breath and lets it out. She turns my desk chair around and sits on it so she's facing me. I'm sitting on my bed.

"He was just a boy." Her face is even more beautiful, I notice, when it's filled with sorrow or nostalgia or longing or whatever it is she's feeling right now. "He was a boy I thought I loved. I mean, I did love him, but where I was wrong, I guess, was in believing that he loved me. Although when I look back at the situation, I'm not so sure he didn't love me." She stops and seems to realize that this isn't the real point here. "It was all very complicated. Too complicated. But here's something simple: his name was Joe."

"Joe."

"Yes. Joe."

"Tell me more. It's all the complicated stuff that's interesting to me." I mean this. I'm pretty well practiced at hearing stories of teenage angst and love and sex, and to think that this story actually involves me is thrilling.

"Yeah. To me too. Okay." A strand of her hair has fallen in her face, and she tucks it behind her ear. "Joe was a Lubavitcher. What that means is that he was a member of this big Hasidic group—the biggest, actually. He was the cousin of a friend of mine from the neighborhood. He lived in Boston. I would go with her sometimes to visit her family, even though my father wasn't a big fan of Chabad."

She's totally losing me. She reads this on my face.

"Chabad is pretty much the same thing as Lubavitcher. Never mind. None of this is important except for you to know that as the oldest daughter of the Rebbe, even though I was only sixteen, my parents already had a pretty good idea about whom I would marry, and I never liked that boy too much. And who was thinking about marriage, anyway? Certainly not me. But Joe was really cute and smart and had these amazing cheekbones, and I was just crazy about him. We started this secret love affair, because not only was he Chabad and not whom my

125

parents had in mind for me, but there really is no such thing as dating among the Hasidim. It's even forbidden for a man and woman, or a boy and a girl like we were, to be in the same room with the door closed unless they're married. But we were kids and fell in love, and the rules didn't matter."

This is starting to sound like Romeo and Juliet but with lots of hair and heavy dark clothes. It strikes me as totally absurd when I conjure up a picture of two bad-ass Orthodox kids breaking all the rules. But then I look at Rivka's face and I can imagine her as just a kid, a kid like me, and I realize that I very easily could have been one of them. If fate hadn't snatched me away, I would have been born into an Orthodox life. Would that mean that I wouldn't have a crazy crush on a guy like Zack Meyers? I don't think so.

"And then, obviously, I got pregnant. Would you believe that it happened on the very first time? Just my luck."

"Jesus."

"Simone, I'm not telling you this as some kind of lesson about abstinence or anything. Sex is great. It's amazing."

"So I've heard."

"Well, you've heard right. And whenever you're ready you should have lots of it. All the time. But be more careful about it than I was. And be more careful about whom you have it with."

I'm turning red. Mom would never talk to me like this. She's very cool and very open, but when it comes to sex she clams up and says something vague about how I need to be responsible, which I've always interpreted to mean: *Don't have sex, but if you do, by all means don't tell me about it.*

"Anyway. Like I said, I loved Joe. When I told him I was pregnant, though, he totally freaked out and basically refused to ever talk to me again. And that really hurt—I mean, it really, really hurt. But in the end it was okay, because I may have been only sixteen, but I knew enough to know that I didn't want to get married, even to Joe. I had no idea what to do. I was lost. I was terrified. I was in total darkness. And then—and I still believe this to this day—God sent me your mother."

Jules disappeared while Rivka and I were up in the attic talking. Now Rivka is on her way back home, probably somewhere on Route 3 heading south toward Cape Cod. I wonder what she's listening to. What kind of music does she like? Or maybe she's listening to NPR? A book on tape? I'm stretched out on the couch in the living room, pretending to read a magazine. Mom and Dad and Jake are in the kitchen cleaning up, and I'm taking advantage of the situation—given everything I've had to deal with today, no one's going to ask me to so much as dry a dish.

I keep turning over Rivka's words in my head. *God sent me your mother*. I realize that a simple comma would change everything. Watch: *God sent me, your mother*. See? But this isn't what Rivka said. She didn't say *God sent me, your mother*. She didn't say *God sent me, Rivka, your mother*. No. She said *God sent me your mother*. She said God sent my mother, Elsie Turner, to her, Rivka Levin, in her time of need. Well, if God was looking out for Rivka, then you kind of have to wonder why he let her get pregnant in the first place, don't you? But then again, if she hadn't gotten pregnant, I wouldn't be here. So maybe God sent *me* my mother. Wait a minute. I don't even believe in God.

I look out the window. The air is thick with fog, and I hope it isn't too difficult to see on the road. I can picture her face illuminated by the headlights of cars carrying people away from Cape Cod back north toward the city.

My family emerges from the kitchen together. A united front. Jake is drying his hands on his jeans. They all find seats in the living room and pretend to do something else as they take turns studying me slowly flipping through the pages of my magazine. Finally Jake can't stand it anymore.

"So?"

I fold the magazine and put it down. They look at me expectantly.

"It wasn't half bad," I say.

And my mom and my dad and my brother all smile their same smile at me.

twelve

WINTER BREAK IS JUST AROUND THE CORNER.
They used to call it "Christmas break" only a few
years ago, but they changed it to the neutral and less
controversial "winter break." The school did this
without pressure from the Atheist Student Alliance
because there was no Atheist Student Alliance at
Twelve Oaks a few years ago. So winter break is just
around the corner, and that's a good thing because
I'm falling behind in my schoolwork. I have this massive history paper due, and I haven't even started.

I don't have time to think about U.S. history. I'm
too busy thinking about *my* history. I hate to admit it,
but Mom and Dad were right. I need to know more. I
have to know more.

I'm a person with a three-pronged story. There's
Mom and there's Dad and there's Rivka. Now that
I've seen her face, I can't continue to pretend that she

isn't part of who I am. My story has three prongs, not four, because Joe was just some boy who is gone. Vanished. Evaporated. He isn't even a ghost. He's nothing. Anyway, from what Rivka has heard, he moved to Israel thirteen years ago and doesn't plan on ever coming back. So he might as well not exist, which is irrelevant because, like I already said, he doesn't exist to me anyway.

I've been talking on the phone with Rivka. She invited me to come down to her house on Cape Cod and spend the night and she'll tell me more about her family. I'm going this Friday. I'm taking the Subaru and going by myself. I've never driven that far alone, and I'm kind of excited about that. I thought maybe Mom and Dad would object. They aren't crazy about me driving alone, and also I'm wondering when this whole enthusiasm for my relationship with Rivka might begin to wear out. I know they wanted me to meet her—they pushed me to meet her so that I can know about myself and my story—but they don't want me to make her too big a part of my life, do they? I'm confused. I think if I were in their position I'd feel jealous or threatened, but they just smile and encourage it all and bend over backward to make it easy for me, including breaking their own rules by letting me drive all the way to Wellfleet alone. What can I say? I don't understand my parents.

After coming back from Arizona, Cleo announced that she's never setting foot in the state of Arizona again. She said she doesn't care if that's the last time she lays eyes on Edward. She seems a little wounded that I had such a different reaction to my visit with Rivka, like I'm letting her down by not hating Rivka, by wanting more of a relationship with her. But she's also really happy for me that it went as well as it did and that Rivka's young and pretty and not some freaky religious zealot, which is how Cleo pictured her. Cleo even wanted to go with me this Friday, but I told her maybe next time. I think it's best if I take this drive alone.

There's this big dance on Friday night called the Snow Ball that used to be something Cleo and I made fun of endlessly. But of course Cleo is going this year because she has a boyfriend, and suddenly the Snow Ball isn't so stupid anymore. (You can see that her offer to come with me to Rivka's probably wasn't very serious, so I don't feel too bad about saying no.) And to make matters worse, Jake is going to the Snow Ball with this girl in my class named Sam, who asked him by leaving a note in his locker. Little Jake has a date with a junior! So there's no getting around the fact that I'm just a big old loser. But at least I get to drive by myself to Cape Cod.

*　　*　　*

I want to make something clear. I'm not obsessed. I'm not coming unglued. And I'm not a stalker. But I did happen to overhear Zack Meyers say in our *Gazette* meeting yesterday that he had to work this afternoon, and I decide that after school I should stop by the Organic Oasis and buy a honey-and-fruit-juice-sweetened dessert for my family. Why not? I know Dad is cooking something good for dinner because I saw a white-butcher-paper-wrapped package in the fridge and a large bunch of mixed fresh herbs on the counter. Dad doesn't do desserts, so I decide it would be a nice idea to surprise the family with something from the baked goods section of the Organic Oasis. Okay, so maybe my family deserves better than a dessert sweetened with honey and fruit juice, but isn't it the thought that counts? The Organic Oasis is on my way home. And once I'm there I'll probably get a cup of coffee.

Cleo asks me what I'm doing after school. Jules has loosened the reins a bit, and now Cleo is allowed to talk on the phone again and hang out with her friends, but she's forbidden to have Darius over or to go to Darius's house without parental supervision. I'm surprised that Cleo's still breathing, let alone gaining her freedom. Recently Cleo accused Jules of being so strict because she's jealous that Cleo is having sex when it's obvious that Jules hasn't had sex in a really, really long time. Cleo was laughing when she told me this story. I didn't want to sound like the prude that I obviously am, but if I ever talked to my mother like that, I think the earth would split open and swallow me whole. And I don't just mean that I'd get in huge trouble, which I most definitely would. I mean that the idea of a daughter speaking to her mother this way disrupts my sense of the order of the universe. But it's different with Cleo and Jules. I think when you're alone together for all those years, just a mother and a daughter, you learn to function with your own set of rules in your own language.

When I tell Cleo I have to stop by the Organic Oasis to pick up a dessert, she gets this knowing look.

"Ahhh. Is a certain barista going to be manning the coffee counter this afternoon?"

"So what if he is?"

"I am *so* going with you."

"And what purpose would that serve exactly?"

"Dual purposes. A, to find out what is up with him and Amy Flannigan, and B, to use my perfectly honed Spidey senses to determine if he's interested in you."

I could come up with a million reasons why she can't go with me, but who am I kidding? I'm powerless over Cleo.

She's waiting at my locker when school gets out.

"Don't you have someplace you can go and do your boyfriend?"

"Don't be crass, Simone." This is pretty funny stuff coming from Cleo. "Darius has practice, and anyway, this is way more important." So off we go to the Organic Oasis.

We park the car and pass the display of fresh flowers and fruits. They look much sadder on this December afternoon clustered together under an awning and a heat lamp. Just as we get to the doors I stop her and grab her arm.

"Cleo, please. Don't embarrass me."

"Who do you think I am, your mother? Don't worry. You're in the hands of a professional."

"No, what I mean is, you know you have a different approach to these things than I do. I'm not as out there as you are. And I don't want to put myself out there. I—"

"You don't want him to know you like him but you still want to know if he likes you."

"This is very sixth-grade of you, but yes."

"No, Simone, this is very sixth-grade of *you*. You have to give him a little something. You can't expect him to show interest in you unless he picks up that you're receptive." The automatic doors are stuck on open and starting to make a strained noise. We step out of the way. I'm out of my league here. I don't know how to play this game, how to show I'm receptive, any of this. Cleo looks at me carefully and her look softens, and I know instantly that she's right, I *am* in the hands of a professional, but more importantly I'm in the hands of someone who has known me my entire life.

"Don't worry," she says. "Come on. Let's go get some coffee."

There he is behind the counter in a chocolate brown apron. He has a row of glass canisters lined up and he's filling them with sugar. Maybe I'm coming unglued after all, but for a moment I think he lights up when he sees me.

"Good afternoon, ladies," he says, and does a little half bow. God, is he adorable or what?

"*Hola*, Zack," says Cleo. "*¿Cómo estás?*" Zack and Cleo are in the same Spanish class.

"*Muy bien. Muy bien.* What can I get for you, Cleo?" I feel my heart sinking. Forget showing him I'm receptive; he doesn't even know I'm here. But then he turns and looks at me. "I know what you like," he says. "You like good old-fashioned all-American no-frills coffee. But your friend Cleo here strikes me as a bit more high-maintenance."

"Ah, Zack, you read me like a book. Gimme a non-fat latte with a shot of vanilla syrup."

We pay for our coffees and take two empty stools

136

at the counter. We're Zack's only customers.

"It's been a painfully slow afternoon," he says. Oh. So when I imagined him lighting up from the sheer joy of seeing me, he was really just expressing relief that someone, anyone, was here to distract him from his afternoon alone with the sugar canisters. "But I've been able to get some good thinking done. For example," he says, "did you ever stop and count exactly how many baseball metaphors there are in the English language?"

"Huh?" Yes, this is what I say. I say "huh" like some kind of Neanderthal.

"There are the obvious ones, like when something's 'a home run' or 'out of the park.' But there are so many more—there's no end to them, really. 'I struck out,' 'He threw me a curve' . . ."

Cleo chimes in. "And don't forget the bases, as in 'I got to second base with him.'"

I should have said that, right? That must be what Cleo means by showing you're receptive.

"Who could forget the bases?" he says, and smiles.

"God, Zack. You must really be bored, or else you must really love baseball."

"I'm guilty of both."

I realize I need to jump into this conversation. I seem lately to have a lock on the role of the mute.

"I never would have pegged you for a baseball

137

fan," I say. "Where's your Red Sox cap? Your baseball card collection?" Not bad, right? Better than "huh," don't you think?

"Both safe and sound at home," he says. "And my card collection truly is impressive, although I have to confess I haven't added to it since I blew my whole bar mitzvah wad on a 1955 mint condition Ted Williams."

A light bulb goes off over Cleo's head. I can see it happen, and I can't move quickly enough to derail what I know is coming next.

"You're Jewish?" she asks. "So's Simone. Well, I mean, she just discovered she's Jewish."

This is a moment when I should feel betrayed by Cleo. Where to begin? For one thing, this is a way too obvious attempt to get Zack's attention. Also, it opens the door to a part of me that is very private and personal. And maybe it's even offensive. But instead of looking confused or affronted or asking me a bunch of questions I don't feel like answering, he just sticks out his hand for me to shake.

"Mazel tov," he says. "Welcome to the tribe."

I smile at him. "Thanks. It's great to be here."

And by the way, his skin is really soft.

Zack gives us free refills and we hang around for another half an hour, during which time Cleo manages to find out that he's not going to the Snow Ball because he's not a big fan of high school dances. When Cleo asks why he isn't taking Amy Flannigan, Zack sighs and rolls his eyes as if he's sick to death of answering that question and says that they are *just friends*. And then he adds that Amy has a boyfriend who's a freshman at UC Berkeley.

So Amy has a boyfriend. Her boyfriend is not Zack Meyers. Therein lies the solution to the Zack and Amy Conundrum. In all my various applications of Z and A, I never factored in BB, the Boyfriend at Berkeley. Cleo was right. She is a professional. She extracted from Zack a snippet of information well worth the price of both our coffees and even her own clumsiness around my newfound Jewish roots. I pick out my dessert, blueberry apricot crumble sweetened with—you guessed it—honey and fruit juice, and I take it home to my deserving family.

It's Friday afternoon. Mom wrote me a note getting me out of seventh period because she wants me to arrive at Rivka's before it gets dark. The car is loaded with way more snack food than anyone should eat in the two hours or so it should take me to get there. Given all the snacks, Mom has gone surprisingly light on the drinks, just a half a bottle of water, and when I point this out she tells me that she's worried that if I drink too much I'll have to pee and she doesn't want me stopping anywhere between here and Wellfleet. I also promise not to talk on my cell phone or to play the music too loud. I promise to stay in the slow lane. She really seems flustered, and I figure this must be about more than just my driving alone, so I try not to get too annoyed with her. Neither Dad nor Jake is around to see me off, and this appears to bother Mom, but I remind her that I'll be back tomorrow, it's not like I'm moving away, and then I see that her eyes are filling with tears. I give her a big hug, get in the car and start it up, then roll down my window and say, "I love you, Mom," which isn't something I'm in the habit of saying all the time, and then I put the car in reverse and back out of our driveway.

Another good thing about getting to leave school early, other than missing physics, is that there's almost no traffic. Maybe this is because it's only three-thirty, or maybe this is because no one goes to Cape Cod in December. Once I get onto 93 I immediately break two of Mom's rules. I pass an old Buick, requiring that I dip into the fast lane. And I turn up the volume on *The Eminem Show* to the point where the bass is rattling the windshield. But when my cell phone rings a few minutes later and I see that it's James, I don't answer it. So I'm one out of three.

Boston has disappeared from my rearview mirror. I've passed the big open concrete lot where every

April the Big Apple Circus sets up its blue and yellow tent. I've passed the JFK Library, where during my third-grade field trip I broke out in the first few tell-tale red bumps of chicken pox. And somewhere in there I must have driven by the community where Rivka grew up and where the rest of the Levins still live.

I'm now on Route 3 going south. This land is flat. The bare-branched skeletons of trees have given way to big bushy pines. I crack my window just a little bit and am pretty sure I can smell the salt from the sea. Fog is settling in, and I've left behind the Massachusetts I know. It's only another few miles to the Sagamore Bridge. This bridge will carry me from the main boxy block of the state onto the curled claw of Cape Cod. It will carry me from my life and my past and all that I know and all that is familiar onto this jutting edge of continent where I have never set foot and where everything is still a mystery.

I think about home. Even though the Snow Ball is a full three hours away, Cleo's probably starting to get ready. She tried her dress on for me last week, and I told her what she needed to hear and what also happened to be the God's honest truth—she looks amazing in it. Jake is refusing to wear a tie. I guess this is just a nod to the fact that he'd prefer to wear nothing at all above the waist. But he has a nice black suit, and Dad bought him a white dress shirt with French cuffs, and I'm sure Sam will die when she comes to the door to pick him up, which is something she has to do because Jake is only a freshman. I look down (only for a minute—my eyes are glued to the road, I promise) to see my torn jeans and my beat-up Adidas and my gray zip-up sweatshirt, and I have to admit that I'm far from Snow Ball material. And now here is the bridge. It's rising out of the fog and presenting itself before me, and I sail right over it.

thirteen

RIVKA'S HOUSE IS PINK. I don't mean Barbie's Dream House pink, but weathered pale pink. It has gray trim, and the light on the front porch and in the windows is glowing a warm yellow. The driveway of tiny stones is crackling under the wheels of my car. Before I turn off the ignition, the front door opens and Rivka is standing there with a sweater draped around her shoulders. She smiles and waves, and I do the same, then motion that she should stay where she is—I can handle my bags myself. The fog has disappeared; it's dusk, and the sky is the color of the house, with some low wispy clouds stretched out just above the horizon.

Her house is on the other side of the road from the ocean. It's a quiet road, lined with trees, and I haven't seen another car since I turned onto it. When I walk up the steps onto her porch I turn around and can see the last light from the sky bouncing off the water.

"Call your mother," she says.

"How many times has she called already?"

"Do you really want to know?"

"Not really, but tell me anyway."

"Four."

I use my cell phone, and at first Mom freaks because she thinks that I'm calling from the car, but I tell her that I'm here, that I'm calling from Rivka's front porch, and that I can see the water from where I'm standing.

"Okay, honey. I love you. Have a nice time. Call before you leave tomorrow."

"You too," I say, and snap the phone closed.

"Come on in." Rivka holds the door open for me.

I take a few steps into the living room and put my bags down. I look around. There's a fire in the fireplace and it's warm in here, and for a minute I feel dizzy. It's like I've stepped into an alternative universe. This could be *my* house. I could just be coming home from school, and those great smells coming from the kitchen would be the dinner that I have here every night, and tonight maybe I'd be eating dinner before going out to the Cape Cod High or Wellfleet High or Whatever High winter dance. And maybe in this alternative universe I would actually have a date.

"Let me show you your room," says Rivka, and this is too much for me to take at just this moment, so I say, "Can we wait on that?" and she seems to understand.

I walk around the house. The living and dining rooms are part of one large open space that looks out into a backyard surrounded on all sides by tall pines. The floors are dark wood, and in front of the fire are two big comfortable couches separated by an old painted coffee table. There's a mug on it and a book with its spine facing up that she must have put down when she heard my car. There's a large photograph of the beach hanging over the fireplace that I immediately recognize as one of Rivka's. I regret the snide comment I made over Thanksgiving about beach photography, because this picture is stunning. Everything seems to be moving: the gray-blue ocean, the low clouds, the impossibly tall electric-green beach grass in the foreground, even the flat sand.

The kitchen is almost the same size as the living and dining area, with a big island in the middle, a small table, and a built-in window seat with striped cushions. A staircase leads from the kitchen up to something, but I don't follow it. It must be Rivka's room. I find a small bedroom with a slanted ceiling just off the living room that turns out to be the room Rivka was going to show me to, my room, but I find it easier to think of it as the guest room. I put my bag on the bed. I put my backpack on a small wooden desk by the window.

"Nice house," I say, and I really mean it. It's rustic and cozy, and I'm happy to find that she isn't one of those people who has doilies everywhere or little porcelain animals or crocheted signs that say WEL-COME FRIENDS.

"Thanks," she says. "I love it here. It's quiet."

I guess if you grew up with six other kids and the whole neighborhood coming and going all the time, you would learn to love quiet too. I listen carefully and can't hear a thing but the gentle crackle of the fire.

"It smells great in here."

"Brisket," she says. "I figured I'd make the classic Friday night dinner. I hope you eat meat."

I love meat. I know I shouldn't but I do. I'm aware it isn't great for you and that it comes from helpless creatures, but like the bumper sticker I saw once on a VW Bug, my favorite bumper sticker of all time, says, if God didn't want us to eat animals, then why did He make them out of meat?

When I tell this to Rivka she laughs heartily. "I think that comes directly from the Torah."

"I'm sure it does."

She glances quickly at her watch. Am I boring her? Does she have somewhere to go?

"It's time to make Shabbat," she says.

Shabbat? I'm not exactly certain what Shabbat is, but I'm pretty sure it's something religious, and I feel a rush of panic and confusion. Didn't she say something about leaving this all behind? Didn't she tell me right to my face that this isn't who she is anymore? I mean, look at her. She doesn't look like a religious freak.

"I'm an atheist," I say quickly.

"Good for you. I admire your strength of conviction. Me? I can't make up my mind, so I like to keep all my options open. I'm more of an agnostic."

"So you're not Jewish?"

"I'm definitely Jewish. But I'm also agnostic. I'm Jagnostic. Or Agnewish."

"I'm confused."

"Obviously I am too."

This isn't helping matters. I need some clarity here.

"So what do you mean by 'It's time to make Shabbat'?" I ask.

She gestures to the dining room table, a country antique with stains and scrapes that has the look of a table that's fed generations of families. There are two candlesticks with short, unlit white candles, a silver cup filled with red wine, a platter with a loaf of bread peeking out from under a white cloth, and a bouquet of tulips in a green glass vase.

"What I mean is it's Friday night. The start of the Jewish Sabbath. Every Friday at sundown I light Shabbat candles, drink wine, and eat challah."

"What do you do with the flowers?"

"Nothing. They just look nice."

I have nothing against candles or wine or bread. In fact, I'm a pretty big fan of all three.

"Simone, I don't want you to feel uncomfortable. This is just something I do every Friday night. You can go hang out in the kitchen or in your room, or you can stand here and stare at me like I'm completely insane. Whatever you want."

"It's okay. I'll watch," I say, because what could possibly be so threatening about candles or wine or bread? Rivka seems like a pretty together person. I don't think she brought me here and went through all this just to try some kind of surprise religious ambush on me.

She takes a pack of matches and lights the candles. Then she takes a deep breath and slowly releases it, stretches her neck to the left and then the right, and drops her shoulders. She's relaxing. I can actually see it happening; I see her letting something go. She lowers her head. Again I notice how quiet it is in here. With a few slow motions she waves the smoke from the candles up toward her face and breathes in the waxy smell of them. She puts her fingertips to her forehead so that her palms are shielding her eyes from the flames. Then she starts to sing quietly in a language I don't know but assume must be Hebrew. It's a melancholy tune, and she has a beautiful singing voice that I clearly didn't inherit from her. She stops, picks up the silver cup of wine, holds it out in front of her, and starts to sing again. I try to imagine what the words mean. It's obviously some kind of prayer, but I'm not bothered by it because I have no idea what it means. In fact, it's having a hypnotic effect on me. Maybe it's the singing coupled with the fire and an afternoon of staring at the white lines on the road. Whatever it is, I haven't touched a drop of the wine, yet I feel a warm buzzing in my head.

Rivka finishes singing, takes a deep drink of the wine, and offers the silver cup to me.

"Thanks," I say. It tastes earthy, like dirt and grass and silver. I realize that doesn't sound so good, but trust me, it's delicious.

She tells me she needs to go wash her hands and she disappears into the kitchen. Apparently this is part of the evening's ritual. When she returns she uncovers two small loaves of bread. I've had challah before, from the Organic Oasis. The crust is always really hard and the inside is a little dry. She holds one up for me to grab, and I do—it's soft to the touch— but she keeps a grip on the other end. She quickly half chants, half sings one last thing in Hebrew and then tears a piece from her end, and I do the same from mine. The challah is chewy and dense and slightly sweet. When I comment on how good it is, Rivka tells me she baked it herself.

"Are you hungry? Should we eat?" she asks.

"That's it?" I ask. "Shabbat's over?"

Rivka laughs. "No, it's just beginning. Shabbat lasts until Saturday at sundown. But now we have to eat brisket. The Lord commands that after you light the candles you must eat brisket with roasted baby new potatoes and braised fennel."

I help set the table, and she brings all the food out from the kitchen. The Shabbat candles are casting a really beautiful glow in the house. We sit down and I wait for her to start serving up the brisket. I'm trying not to salivate openly. But she just sits there for a minute looking at the table and looking at me. She breathes in the smell of the food, the candles, the fire. She pours the wine from the silver cup into a real wineglass, swirls it around, and takes a sip.

"I'm so grateful to have you here," she says.

"Thanks," I say. I feel my cheeks getting warm. I look down at my empty plate. "I'm glad to be here too."

Everything tastes as good as it smells, and again I ponder the unexplored talents that may lie within me. I've never spent much time in the kitchen except for the occasional chopping and peeling. The kitchen is Dad's turf. But now I'm thinking I should start paying attention to what he does in there because if Rivka's a good cook, maybe I could be one too, maybe even better than Dad.

"Tell me more about Shabbat." I'm trying to figure out why she bothers with all this if she isn't living in the Hasidic community anymore.

"Shabbat is really important to me still," she says. "It is a way to separate out a part of my life, a time in the week when I slow down and appreciate the things around me. I sit down to a meal with family or friends and try not to let anything intrude on this sacred space."

This makes perfect sense. It sounds nice. It sounds like what happens in my house, at my dinner table, almost every night, and I feel a rush of appreciation for Mom and Dad and Jake.

"I've given up much of the hard-core restrictions we had growing up," she continues. "For example, I'll run the dishwasher after this meal without any guilt. In my house growing up—in all Orthodox homes— you don't use any electricity, operate any kind of mechanical device, or do any kind of work on Shabbat. So I don't observe it in the strictest sense, but Shabbat has always had deep meaning for me.

I light the candles and do the blessings over the wine and the bread every Friday night, even if I'm all by myself, which I am quite frequently."

I make a mental note to come back to this issue of her being alone. Was she ever married? Did she ever live with anyone? Is there anyone in her life now? But before I get to the bottom of this I still need to understand her relationship with someone else. I need to understand her relationship with the Man upstairs.

"I don't get it," I say. "You said you're agnostic. That means you don't know if God exists, right? Well, then, why do you bother praying to Him every Friday night?"

"Saying those blessings is more about tradition to me than religion. I do it because it's what Jews do. It's part of the Jewish tradition. And tradition gives me a sense of my place in the world. It defines me. Whether or not God exists doesn't matter that much to me in the end, I guess. I've lived moments on both sides, moments where God is nowhere to be found and moments where God is so close I can almost reach out and touch Him."

She pours me a little bit of wine without even asking if I want any. This makes me feel grown-up, like we're two friends talking and enjoying our meal. Like we aren't an adult and a child. Like we aren't a mother and a daughter.

"So tell me about your family. Go back as far as you can. But hold on a minute," I say, and get up from my seat. "I need to get my notebook."

She tells me about her great-grandparents in Russia and her grandparents, who came to America in their twenties. She tells me about Mordechai as a young boy and Hannah as a young girl. I've filled five pages with notes. It's getting late. The wine has gone to my head. The Shabbat candles have burned down to almost nothing, and still I'm transfixed—I can't keep my eyes off them until finally the one on the left goes out and a tall plume of black smoke rises from it, snapping me back into the moment. I ask about her parents and her siblings now. Where are they? What are they doing?

Rivka yawns and rubs her eyes. She stretches her arms high above her head. "Maybe we can save the rest for breakfast, if you don't mind. Remember, I have six brothers and sisters. There's a lot of ground to cover. A lot has happened." Now she's staring at the remaining candle's barely flickering flame. "My mother died five years ago."

"I'm sorry," I say, and I am. I don't know much about Hannah, but I have a feeling I would have liked her. And now she's gone. She'll never be anything but a character in a story—in *my* story.

I get up and take the last few dishes into the kitchen. Rivka is still sitting at the table.

"Well," I say, "I guess I'll go to bed."

She looks up at me. "Simone?"

"Yes?"

"I have a favor to ask you," she says. She looks sorrowful. Apologetic. A little nervous. "There's a blessing I skipped over. I've always wanted to do it and I've never been able to, but I could do it tonight with your permission."

I just stare at her, waiting for her to say more.

"There's a blessing that comes between the candles and the wine. A blessing you say over your child. I've always wanted to say this blessing, to bless you. I've thought about it every Shabbat since you were born. May I?"

"Of course," I say, and she stands up and comes over to me and puts her hands on my head. They are warm and heavy on me. She closes her eyes. I close mine and feel all the people, all the past, all the slowly unfolding mysteries rushing through me. I take a deep breath. Rivka begins to whisper in this new language I've heard many times tonight, this language that is beginning to sound familiar to my ears.

fourteen

I'M A FITFUL SLEEPER. I often wake up with my pillows on the floor and the sheets in a tangle around my ankles, and sometimes my head winds up where my feet were when I shut off the light. But this morning I wake up with my head on two pillows and crisp sheets still perfectly tucked beneath the mattress. I don't think I even have a hair out of place. Maybe it was the wine. Maybe it was the fresh sea air. Maybe it was Rivka's blessing. Whatever it was, I am refreshed and clearheaded and happy to be here and happy to be alive.

When I find Rivka sitting in the kitchen, she has the look of someone who woke up in a tangle of sheets with the pillows on the floor, if she even went to sleep at all. She's hunched over a mug of coffee. There are dark circles under her eyes, and her face looks drawn and pale.

"Good morning," I say.

She smiles weakly. "Did you sleep well?"

"Extremely. You?"

"Not so much."

"That's too bad," I say. "I wonder why."

She runs her hands through her hair. "Simone, I have something to tell you." She reaches her leg under the kitchen table and pushes out the chair across from her. She motions for me to have a seat.

I stand right where I am, in the doorway. My mind is racing. This feels like one of those moments when you know that there are only a few seconds separating you in your state of blissful ignorance from some new knowledge that is going to change you forever. And those seconds go by in slow motion. *Tick. Tock. Tick. Tock.* But what could Rivka possibly have to tell me? That I'm adopted? That she's my mother? Maybe she's going to tell me that she's not who I think she is, that she's *not* my mother. Wait a minute. Did something happen at home? Is everyone in my family okay? Is something wrong with Mom or Dad or Jake? No, that can't be. I would have heard the phone ring.

I've been through this before. I've had my fair share of these moments, these conversations, in my life. And I'm still standing in the doorway staring at her when it hits me. Suddenly it all makes perfect sense. Why she found me *now*. Why my parents have been pushing me so hard to get to know her *now*.

"You're sick, aren't you?"

She looks down and studies her coffee mug. I don't even need to hear the answer to my question, but she gives it to me anyway. "Yes," she says. "I am."

I don't really know what it is that I'm feeling. Betrayed? Why would I feel betrayed? It's not like she ever lied to me. I haven't known her for very long, and all things considered, she's telling me this pretty much right up front. Sad? Like I just said, I haven't known her for very long, so how sad can the thought of losing her be? I've lived my entire life without her. Still, I feel something that's keeping me from taking that seat across from her at the kitchen table.

I turn around and go back to the guest room and start to pack, bunching my clothes into balls and jamming them into my bag. I zip it up and toss it onto the desk next to my backpack. The bed hardly needs making because I slept so soundly, but instead of smoothing out the wrinkles, I find myself tearing off the sheets. I throw the pillows across the room. I toss aside the comforter, and it knocks the bedside lamp onto the floor. I'm *angry*. That's what I'm feeling. I'm incensed, not insensate. Why does my life always seem to get more and more complicated? It finally felt like I was resolving something. I was

157

healing something. I was letting some light into the darkest part of me.

And now this.

I storm back into the kitchen. Rivka is just where I left her. She looks so tired and sad and so much less beautiful right now, and I lose some of the steam that powered me in here. When I begin to speak I think I'm going to yell, but instead I sound like a prepubescent boy whose voice is just beginning to crack.

"Why did you bother? Why did you want to meet me?"

She opens her mouth as if she's about to answer, but then she closes it again.

"Don't you think you're being selfish?" I ask her. "I understand you might want to tie up loose ends or get some kind of closure or whatever it is people do at times like this, but did you stop and think about what this would be like for me?"

"Of course I did, Simone. You're all I thought about. Believe me, I wish it weren't this way. I wish it weren't now. But I didn't want you to come to a point in your life when you wanted to know about me and to know about your past and then find that I wasn't around to give you the answers. Maybe you would never have sought me out—I don't know. But I didn't want to take that chance. This is your opportunity, Simone. It's the only opportunity you will have. And

I'm sorry if it came before you're ready."

I walk over to the empty chair and sit down. I take a quick check of myself. Betrayed? No. Angry? A little, but I'm having a hard time hanging on to it because I'm not sure who or what to be angry with. Rivka? Fate? God? Modern medicine? Also, you'd be surprised how satisfying it is to knock over a lamp. When all else fails, take your anger out on inanimate objects. Sad? Yes. Look at Rivka. She's so young, and under that worried expression and the dark circles brought on by a sleepless night, she is vibrant and beautiful. How can she be sick?

"How sick are you?"

"Really sick."

"Oh."

As I look at her sitting there, our first conversation on the telephone comes back to me, and I think about how hard I tried to picture her and where she was and what her kitchen looked like, and now here she is, sitting at her kitchen table, probably right where she was sitting when I was on the other end of the phone. The walls are painted a robin's egg blue. Little potted cactuses line the counter above the sink. I look out the kitchen window and see that her view is to the south, down the long tree-lined country road.

"You were right to push this on me," I say. "I don't

know when it would have happened exactly, but I'm sure one day I would have come looking for you. I wouldn't have been able to avoid you forever."

"I have to confess, Simone, it wasn't only for your own good. You're right. I am selfish. I really wanted to get to know you. For me. For my own good. And I'm so glad I did." She makes a move as if she is about to reach for my hand, but then she seems to change her mind. "Now can we drop all this morbid crap and enjoy a good breakfast? I have a favorite diner I'd love to take you to."

The diner is called the Briar Patch, and our waitress is this awesome older woman in a pink uniform and crazy blue eye shadow with a name tag that says DOLORES and a voice like Marge Simpson's. When I order my fried eggs and toast she shouts at me—I mean she really shouts at me—"*Any meat,*" without an inflection to make it sound like a question, and this gives both Rivka and me the giggles.

The coffee is atrocious and the orange juice is watery and the booth is sticky, but I totally love this place. Everyone in here looks like they eat here every morning at exactly this time sitting in exactly the same spot having exactly the same breakfast.

"Why don't you have any pictures of them?" I ask. I looked everywhere in her house. I looked on all the walls on every surface in every room. I even snuck a quick look up in Rivka's bedroom when she was outside getting more firewood. I couldn't find one picture.

She pauses for a minute and thinks about it.

"Oh. You mean my family. I do have pictures, but I keep them in a drawer. It's too hard for me to have them out and look at them all the time."

"Why? What happened?"

"There's no simple answer to that."

"I don't need simple answers."

"I guess you could say I lost faith. In God, in that way of life, in my father, in everything. And when I needed a change and to find my own way and my own answers, there wasn't room for me in their lives anymore."

"None of them? What about your brothers and sisters? What about Hannah?"

Rivka waves the coffeepot away when Dolores comes to refill us. "I became this pariah to everyone but my mother. They all treat me differently, like I'm some stranger. Like I'm the weird one. But at least they'll still talk to me. Only my brother Ephraim has completely written me off. He actually sat shiva for me. Not even Mordechai did that."

"What does that mean?"

"Sorry. Right. Sometimes I forget that not everyone

161

was a Hasid in a former life. Sitting shiva is what you do when someone in your family dies. It is a mourning ritual. Ephraim is a fanatic. When I left the community and their way of life, he announced that I was dead to him."

"That seems extreme."

"You could say that."

"So what did Mordechai do?"

"He stopped inches short of sitting shiva. He barely speaks to me or looks at me whenever I go and visit. It's funny—he had a far more extreme reaction to my leaving than he did to my becoming pregnant."

"Wait a minute. I thought Mordechai didn't know you were pregnant. I thought Hannah helped you hide it from him."

"She did help me, and we did hide it. We never spoke of it. Not once. But I know that he knew. I just know it. He made the choice to look the other way. And I think I've never forgiven him for that. In the end, I think that's probably why I had to leave. Because I needed a father, especially at a time like that, and he couldn't be my father. He was always just the Rebbe."

I don't want to argue with her, and I certainly don't want to be thrust into the position of defending Mordechai because I don't know him and from what

I've heard about him I don't think he's someone I'd like to spend my time defending, but it seems to me that Rivka's logic on this is a little faulty. If Mordechai were really just being the Rebbe, he wouldn't have looked the other way. He would have kicked Rivka out of the house. He would have disowned her. He would have done everything Rivka feared he would do when she went to my mother for help.

Dolores delivers our plates like it's a big inconvenience for her. I still don't have a fork, but Rivka doesn't wait for me. She digs right in. I appreciate this about her. She's comfortable enough around me to drop her manners. Would I wait for Cleo's fork to come if we were having breakfast together at a diner? No way. I watch Rivka devouring her pancakes like a ravenous and perfectly healthy person. How can she be sick? Sick people don't eat pancakes like that. I want to ask what's wrong with her. What is she sick with? How long is she going to live? But I'm not sure how you ask a question like that of someone who seems to be enjoying her pancakes so much.

So we talk about nothing. We talk about everything but what is right there on the table between us. I tell her about school and my friends, and I even tell her about my crush on Zack. And then I use Zack as a segue into asking if she has a boyfriend. She just says no without elaborating. So I ask if she has ever been married, and she says, "God, no."

Then she seems to realize that her answers are too clipped, so she adds, "I always imagined that I'd get married in my forties. I guess it was a reaction to my mother and looking at the life of someone who got married before she knew anything about herself." She slowly stirs her cold coffee. She looks up at me. "But I want you to know that I've had many good relationships since my first one with Joe, and some have even ended well, with lasting friendships."

"I guess all high school romances are doomed to disaster."

"It'll be different with you," she says. "You seem so much more together than I ever was. So much more sure of yourself. So much stronger. You should have far better luck with guys than I ever did."

"You don't think it takes strength to leave everything you know and everyone you love to discover a life on your own? I don't think I could ever do that. And as for my luck with guys, sometime when we aren't eating breakfast, remind me to tell you the making-out-and-puking story that made me famous at my school."

Even though I protest, Rivka will not allow me to pay for breakfast. She says that it's been a good year for beach photography and this one is most definitely on her. So I release the bill from my grip and let her plop down the whopping $9.49.

On the drive back to her house I stare out the window. It is extraordinarily beautiful here. I can understand not only why Rivka would choose to live here but also why she would choose this landscape as the foundation of her work.

"I hope I gave you enough information," she says as we pull into her driveway. "I know we got into some other stuff, and that kind of took time away from the Levin family saga."

This is the only reference either of us has made to her illness since our conversation this morning. Again I feel like I should say something about it, but I simply can't.

"I'll be counting on you for more next time."

"I'll be counting on you counting on me," she says.

I load the car while Rivka makes me a brisket sandwich for the road. She also packs some grapes and almonds and ginger cookies. Doesn't anyone realize that I'm not going to starve during a two-hour drive? That I'd be fine with a stick of gum? Rivka is looking through the windows of the Subaru as if to make sure that no one is stowing away with me, hitching a free ride north. I survey her house and her land and take one last deep breath of the pine trees and the salty air and the wood smoke pouring out of chimneys I can't see but know can't be too far away. There's an awkward pause, and then Rivka leans over and gives me a hug, and I pat her on the back a little too hard. She pulls away. She reaches out her hand and quickly touches my cheek. "Drive safely."

I slide in behind the wheel and just sit there. I watch Rivka walk up the front steps and onto the porch. She doesn't look back. I watch her close the big wooden door behind her. I watch her shape pass by the front window. I buckle my seat belt and adjust my rearview mirror. But before I start the car and begin the drive back to my home and my family and my life, I make good on my promise: I pick up my phone and call my mother.

fifteen

BEFORE SCHOOL LETS OUT FOR WINTER BREAK
two huge things happen: the Atheist Student Alliance
gets kicked off campus, and Darius kisses another girl
at a party. Obviously, to Cleo, one event is far more
important than the other. I'm not sure she even
remembers that I'm a member of the ASA, and she
certainly doesn't care if the group can meet on campus or not, especially in light of her current drama.
But anyway, both events happen right before school
lets out for winter break.

Let us first examine the ejection of the ASA from
campus.

The Evil Bitch was true to her word. It turns out
she was elected to the school board back in
November by a unanimous vote. You kind of have to
wonder: A, who are these cowards on the school
board? And B, don't they know an Evil Bitch when

they see one? It turns out the answers here are A, rich parents with tons of money and no day jobs, and B, no, they don't. Anyway, her first action was to make a motion that the Atheist Student Alliance be banned from meeting, organizing, or otherwise conspiring to do the devil's work within the confines of the Twelve Oaks campus. Like her election, the vote was unanimous.

Heidi broke the news to us at our last Tuesday meeting before vacation and suggested that when we return in January we meet at the Friendly's on Ridge Road until springtime, when we can meet outside. We all agreed to fork over enough money for a Coke or a milk shake or french fries or something every other Tuesday, buying ourselves the right to take over a few booths in the late afternoon. Heidi said there's no point in fighting this, that it isn't worth the time. We will never win.

After my initial fury and a long debate with Mom, I've come around to agreeing that not only will we not win this battle, but also that we *shouldn't* win this battle. The school is actually right. If the school has a policy that no religious groups are allowed to meet on campus, which is a good solid policy, then they shouldn't grant that privilege to an organization that is devoted to a particular view on religion, such as the ASA. It's kind of like the town seal. Because the town seal has a cross on it, the symbol of the Christian faith, and no other religious symbol, it appears as if the town is endorsing and promoting Christianity. If Twelve Oaks Academy forbids all religious groups from meeting on campus yet allows a group of student atheists to meet, then it appears as if the school is endorsing and promoting atheism.

I only wish that this decision had come earlier and didn't arise out of the vengeful actions of the triumphant and all-powerful Evil Bitch. I am no match for her. She defeats me at every turn.

So, about Darius and this other girl. The actual act, The Kiss, happened back in November over Thanksgiving when Cleo was sunning herself by her father's pool in Arizona. Miraculously, it took almost three and a half weeks before Cleo found out. This time lag makes it worse for Cleo because she's convinced that everyone has known about it for weeks and everyone has been talking about her, pitying her, and laughing at her behind her back.

The other girl's name is Vanessa. Lucky for her she doesn't go to Twelve Oaks because, oddly, the brunt of Cleo's rage is directed at Vanessa, not at Darius. If Cleo were to come face to face with this Vanessa, she might beat the crap out of her. At least this is what she keeps saying. So I told Cleo that I thought she could definitely win in a showdown against Vanessa because all she'd have to do is fire the torpedoes that are camouflaging themselves as her breasts, and I learned that there are times when even a good boob joke doesn't do the trick. It just annoyed her.

So the Cleo and Darius Saga is perched on the edge of a cliff. She hasn't decided what to do with him. Darius's defense is exactly what you might imagine: that he was at a party, he was drunk, he couldn't think clearly, she came on to him, he could have gone farther but stopped himself. I don't know why he thought adding that last part about stopping himself would gain him any ground with Cleo, but I guess guys are pretty clueless. Especially Darius. How many times over Thanksgiving weekend did Cleo tell me she missed him? I know she feels like a fool because he obviously wasn't missing her enough to keep from going to some party and making out with some other girl.

To my shock and surprise, Darius is bending over backward in his effort to smooth things over with Cleo. I even saw him trying to hold her hand between classes. If you'd asked me, I would have guessed that he'd take this opportunity to lose the ball and chain, but instead he seems to be really worried that she's going to break up with him. Not so worried that he doesn't walk around school with that cocky look on his face all day, but he cornered me after school when no one was around, and I know this sounds crazy, but it looked like he was going to cry. I could have told this to Cleo. I could have told her that Darius came to me to get my advice about what he should do, saying that he knew I knew her better than anyone and please wasn't there anything I could do to help him out, but for some reason I chose not to tell Cleo any of this. I didn't tell her because I think she should break up with him. His kissing Vanessa just fulfilled all of my predictions about what kind of boyfriend Darius would be, and I don't believe that this other side of Darius is real.

But then Cleo arrives on my doorstep about a week after learning about The Kiss, and she has this huge grin on her face and some flakes in her hair from the light snow that's been falling all afternoon. She looks as if she could burst into song.

"He told me he loves me."

"What?"

"You heard me."

I grab her and drag her inside, and we make ourselves some chocolate milk and take two glasses up to the attic.

"He loves me. He said so. And you won't believe it, but he actually cried. He said, 'I love you, Cleo,' and then he cried."

"Really," I say. "Jeez, Cleo. I thought no one cares

about love or being in love anymore. I thought love didn't matter."

Cleo looks a little hurt. I'm sure this isn't how she thought I'd react. Here we are sitting on my bed drinking chocolate milk like a picture from the 1950s. Just two high school girls sitting around talking about boys and love. All we're missing are the poodle skirts and bobby socks. I know I'm supposed to say "Wow, you are so lucky" or "That's really neat" or something stupid like that, but instead I throw back in her face her callous words about how no one cares about love. I stop and think about how I must sound. I sound like the jealous friend who doesn't have a boyfriend. I sound like the jealous friend who has never had a boy tell her that he loves her.

"So what did you say?"

"That I love him too. And I do. I think that in the end this was a good thing for us. I think he needed to have this experience, to kiss that little slut at the party, so that he could wake up and realize that he loves me."

Cleo looks so happy sitting there with her chocolate milk mustache. She looks so happy that I find it hard to maintain my skepticism or even my jealousy. After all, I'm not the one who said love didn't matter, and I'm happy to learn that the antilove era is over. I just hope that Darius knows how lucky he is.

I decide that to commemorate this day, to remember Cleo and how happy she looks right at this moment, I'm going to make her a T-shirt in brown with white lettering across the front that says GOT CHOCOLATE MILK?

We aren't a skiing family. We don't go to tropical islands. We most definitely don't go to Disney World. We hang around the house over winter break, sleeping late, going to the movies, eating too much, and doing a lot of nothing. It isn't just Jake and me. Mom's office closes down between Christmas and New Year's. Dad doesn't spend any time in his studio working because I guess no one is in the mood for political cartoons when Santa Claus comes to town. Or maybe it's just that he likes the time at home with Mom. Anyway, Christmas is still a week away, but we're talking about it over dinner tonight, mostly because Dad is fixated on cooking a goose and he's trying to rally our support. Leave it to Dad to talk about one meal just as we're sitting down to another.

Then Mom unfolds her napkin, looks at me, and asks, "Why don't you invite Rivka to join us?"

"I don't think she celebrates Christmas, Mom. It might be kind of weird for her."

"Why wouldn't she celebrate Christmas?" asks my slow-witted little brother.

"Because she's Jewish, you idiot."

"So?"

I look to Mom. "Can you explain this?"

I think Jake senses that he's about to be talked down to, so he tries to preempt it. "Everyone celebrates Christmas. It's an American tradition. Like the Fourth of July. I really doubt it would be weird for her. The goose may be a little weird, but Christmas? What's weird about Christmas?"

"What's weird about Christmas is that it's not a Jewish holiday. It's a Christian holiday. As in *Christ*-mas. And Rivka is *Jew*-ish." I say this very slowly.

"Well, if it's a Christian holiday, then why do *we* celebrate it?"

He's got me there. I wish he'd wipe that huge, self-satisfied grin from his face.

Dad tries to rescue me. He turns to Jake and says, "Christmas is a holiday with Christian roots, but over time it has evolved into a secular holiday for many people like us. You can celebrate Christmas like we do, with a tree and presents, and stop at that and it never feels like a religious holiday. But I think what Simone is saying is that for someone who comes from a strong religious tradition that is not a Christian one, then Christmas is a holiday that belongs to someone else."

I nod noncommittally. I've always loved Christmas.

I love the way the house smells when the tree is up. I love Christmas stockings with all the little things Mom finds to stuff them with. I love the star sweeper at the top of our tree—this ancient stuffed doll of a little boy in green overalls holding a broom trailing a string of tiny silver stars. I even like the stupid Santa hat Dad wears every Christmas morning when he hands out the gifts. Christmas has always been a family holiday, just like Thanksgiving. But now that I think about how the day excludes someone like Rivka, I realize that no matter how many secular symbols you choose to adopt and no matter how many religious symbols you choose to reject, there is no escaping the fact that Christmas is a holiday for Christian people.

Mom leaves the table and returns with a calendar. "Hanukah overlaps with Christmas this year. We could invite Rivka and celebrate both."

I'm not sure how this idea solves my immediate crisis of faith about the holiday. How can I, an avowed atheist, celebrate a holiday that commemorates the birth of Christ? But at least Mom's suggestion solves the problem of how to invite Rivka here to be with us, which is something I would like to do.

When I call Rivka to see if she wants to come, she laughs at the way I trip over myself.

175

"When we celebrate Christmas it's not like we sit around praising Jesus all night. But we usually have Christmas carols on the stereo even though the words don't have much meaning to us. And we have a Christmas tree. But we can also celebrate Hanukah and I want you to come and feel comfortable, and I don't want you to feel left out."

"Simone, please don't worry about it. I'd love to come. But tell me, what's a Christmas tree?"

"What? You don't know what a Christmas tree is?"

"Of course I do. I'm just messing with you."

"I'm glad you can take pleasure in how uncomfortable this whole thing makes me."

"Why would this make you uncomfortable?" she asks me. "You shouldn't feel apologetic about your family traditions. Why shouldn't you celebrate Christmas?"

"Because we aren't real Christians."

"I don't think you have to be a practicing Christian to celebrate the holiday, but then again, this isn't my area of expertise. The only thing I find weird is when Jews celebrate Christmas, and believe me, many of them do. But I have no problem celebrating Christmas with people who aren't Jewish."

Then I ask her something that has been on my mind since the night in Wellfleet, something that I started thinking about during Shabbat.

"Aren't I Jewish?" I ask. "I did some research about Judaism, and I read that anyone born of a Jewish mother is automatically Jewish."

I can hear Rivka shifting her position. Maybe she's moving from the dining room table to one of those cozy couches by the fire.

"Technically speaking, yes, I suppose you are. But I knew when I gave you to Elsie and Vince that you wouldn't be raised as a Jew. Even though this was difficult, especially for my mother, we also knew that they would be wonderful, loving parents, and that was more important than anything else."

"You didn't really answer my question."

"Oh, I think I did. Again, yes, in the strictest of Jewish law, you're considered a Jew because you were born to a Jewish mother. If you want to move to Israel, you can get automatic citizenship. If Hitler were alive today, he wouldn't hesitate to send you off to a concentration camp. But I think being Jewish is about more than to whom you are born. I think it's about the choices you make. I think being Jewish is about your personal relationship to the history, the rituals, the tradition, and the culture of Judaism."

Okay. I have no relationship to any of these things, so I guess what Rivka is saying is that I'm not really Jewish. Which is fine by me. But we *are* going to celebrate Hanukah in our house this year, and I did just have my first Shabbat, so I don't know, maybe things are starting to change.

Anyway. About Rivka. About her illness. About how sick she really is and how long she's going to live.

Rivka has ovarian cancer.

I learned this from Mom. I still haven't mustered up the courage to talk to Rivka directly about it, and I worry that she takes this to mean that I don't care about her, but what can I do? I'm a coward. So instead I went to my mom to find out everything I can't bring myself to ask Rivka.

The technical name for what she has is epithelial ovarian carcinoma. And it isn't good. She's had several courses of aggressive treatment, and it's becoming clear that nothing is working. Even though she seems okay now and even though she looks young and vibrant and beautiful, she is going to die.

This is terrible. It is wrong. And what I'm about to say is shameful, but it's true: I can't stop thinking that I'm going to get cancer too. I'm going to get cancer because Rivka is my mother and I'm her daughter and isn't this kind of thing hereditary? I have Rivka's eyes. I have her voice. She's left-handed. We both have sensitive skin. It turns out we're both allergic to walnuts. Am I going to get ovarian cancer?

Then there's the matter of Hannah. Rivka said she

died five years ago. Hannah was not an old woman five years ago. But Mom tells me that Hannah died of a brain aneurysm, not ovarian cancer. I'm not really sure if this information is supposed to soothe me or to make me worry that I could die of a brain aneurysm *or* ovarian cancer, whichever finds me first.

Mom has done quite a bit of research on both and tells me that even though I'm at a higher risk of getting ovarian cancer or having a brain aneurysm than your average person, the odds are still extremely low.

I can't help but think about the benefits to my life before. The benefits of knowing nothing. The benefits of having a bare, solitary trunk for a family tree rather than a tree that is growing more leaves and limbs day by day.

sixteen

THE WEATHER OUTSIDE IS FRIGHTFUL. And if Dad had listened to Mom and called the guy to come fix our flue instead of trying to do it himself, we would have a fire that would be so delightful. But Dad is stubborn, and we're relying on our oil burner in the basement to keep the house warm. Rivka made it here just in time. Only about ten minutes after she parked her car behind the Subaru in the driveway, the snow started coming down hard, in sheets of fast-moving white confetti. The house smells of goose. I'm sure you have no idea what goose smells like, and I hate to rely on a cliché, but it smells just like chicken.

I have to make a confession. I've made a daily trip to the Organic Oasis for a cup of no-frills coffee each morning during this first week of winter break. Each morning my heart rate tripled when I walked in and saw Zack behind the counter. I figure this is as good as going to the gym and doing cardio. I can't get Cleo's voice out of my head. I don't want Zack to know that I go there for coffee because his hair has gotten shaggier and his cheeks are even redder in the wintertime, which in turn make his eyes look particularly green behind his adorable glasses, but on the other hand, I do want to appear receptive if he happens to decide that he's interested in me. This is all way too complicated and I'm sure I'm bungling the whole thing, but some of these mornings we just got to talking, and when I wasn't focusing too much on what he might be thinking about me or whether or not I was appearing receptive to what he must be thinking about me, we actually had a lot to say to each other.

I asked Zack about Christmas and if he celebrates it. He said absolutely, that he celebrates Christmas every year without fail. It's a family tradition. Every Christmas he and his older brother and his parents go to a matinee and then out for Chinese food at Ah Fong's on State Street. That is Zack's Christmas. No tree. No Santa Claus. Just a movie and some lo mein. I asked him if he'd ever been to anyone else's house for Christmas and if so, was he uncomfortable? He gave me a funny look and said, "Simone, are you inviting me over to your house for Christmas?"

Well, that was pretty much the end of my cool façade. I turned red. I sputtered. And then I blurted out, "No!" much more forcefully than I meant to, and he said that he was just joking, and then I told him all about the Rivka Situation and how she's coming to our house for Christmas and how I want to make sure that she feels comfortable, and he said something like "Wow, what an amazing story."

I really regret the way I shouted no, because even though I wasn't inviting him over for Christmas and even though I don't want him to think that I was inviting him over for Christmas, I also don't want him to think that I think inviting him over to my house is a repulsive idea, which might have been the impression I left him with by shouting no.

So the tree is up and the star sweeper is perched on top, surveying a huge pile of presents. As I mentioned, Dad's goose is in the oven, and we are listening to the sound track to the old CBS television special *A Charlie Brown Christmas*. It's melancholy and beautiful and not overtly Christmas-like, so I think it's a good choice for Rivka. Mom bought a menorah, and I looked at the calendar and noted that tonight is the sixth night of Hanukah, so I already have it set up on the mantel over the fireplace, above the stockings, with six candles plus the middle one you use to light the others, which is called the shammes candle (I learned this on the Web. What did people do before the Internet?), so that makes a total of seven candles.

I'm sort of embarrassed when Rivka reaches into her bag and removes her own menorah. Did she think I'd forget? Didn't I tell her that we'd celebrate Hanukah tonight? Does she think I'm so clueless about Judaism that I couldn't figure out that to celebrate Hanukah you need a menorah and candles? When I point out that I already have one, she just says that's great. Then she sees the skepticism on my face.

"This menorah belonged to my mother's parents. They got it as a wedding gift. I light it every night of Hanukah, no matter where I am." She looks at it proudly and puts her hand on my shoulder. "You know, with menorahs and Hanukah, the more the merrier."

I look at it up on the mantel next to the bright shiny copper menorah my mother bought. Ours looks new and tacky. It screams, *Hi. I'm a menorah. I know you aren't Jewish and you have never used me before, but let me help you get through your very first Hanukah!* Rivka's menorah is made of heavy iron with fine carvings of birds and trees and fruits on it. It has permanent dried wax drippings of many different colors from what are clearly decades of Hanukahs. Rivka puts seven candles in her menorah and then steps back and surveys the mantel with a smile.

"Jake," she says, "would you step outside and see if you can count three stars? Once there are at least three stars in the sky, we can light the menorahs."

Jake grabs his parka and seems really happy to take up the task, like he's the man for the job. I think Jake is feeling a little left out of this whole Hanukah thing and is glad to have a role that belongs just to him.

It's a quiet Christmas Eve. Some years we have more family here. My aunt and uncle and cousins from Sag Harbor. My aunt from California. My grandmother used to come, but she died three years ago. Jules and Cleo are often here, but this year they decided to stay home and Darius is supposed to come over for dessert, which is going to be the first time he's come face to face with Jules since that fateful afternoon in Cleo's room. But tonight is a chance for Jules and Darius to get a fresh start, and Cleo is just excited that she's spending Christmas Eve with her boyfriend. James was here last year and I invited him again, but he decided to spend the evening with his family. Last year he hated them all. This year it seems like things are better. They weren't too pleased when he first came out to them, but now I think they understand that this isn't something that's going to change no matter what they do or tell him to do, or no matter how many cute girls his father tries to point out to him in the Twelve Oaks yearbook. So in my house this Christmas Eve, on this sixth night of Hanukah, it's just our little nuclear family. And Rivka.

Jake comes back in the house. His hair is white with snow, and he even has some flakes perched on his unusually long eyelashes. He shakes his head, and snow lands all over the entryway. He wipes his nose on his parka.

"I can't see a thing out there. Forget about stars—I can't even see the house across the street. It's a blizzard."

Rivka hurries over to Jake, takes his coat from him, and hangs it up on the hook in the hallway, like she's welcoming him into her house. He's blowing on his hands to get them warm.

"I'm so sorry, Jake. I wasn't thinking about the snow. I didn't mean to send you out into the elements like that."

"Don't worry about it. I love snowstorms."

"If you can't see stars, can you still light the menorah?" I ask.

"Of course you can. I don't think the three-stars rule is rooted in any ancient Jewish text or anything;

185

it's just what we used to do in our house when I was growing up. We were always so eager to light the candles that my parents had to come up with something to keep us from asking every ten seconds if it was time yet."

I go into the kitchen to get Mom and Dad. They are engaged in something extremely complicated and have the look of two people who are in way over their heads. There are three frying pans on the stove. They are holding two spatulas each. A drop of hot oil just landed on my wrist and I'm still standing in the doorway, so I can only imagine what kind of pain is being inflicted upon them as they stand inches from the stovetop.

"What's going on in here?" I ask.

"Latkes," Dad shouts without looking up from the stove. "Lots and lots of latkes."

Mom rolls her eyes. Clearly this isn't the first time tonight he's made the extremely lame "lots of latkes" joke. I move closer and see that there are little pancakes of shredded potatoes frying in the pans and a whole stack next to the stove on the counter.

"It's time to light the Hanukah candles."

"This is the last batch." Dad is still shouting even though I'm standing right next to him. "We're in the home stretch. Wait for us."

Mom and Dad emerge from the kitchen a few

minutes later beaming, their aprons stained with oil. Mom turns off *A Charlie Brown Christmas* and also the lights from the tree, as if to eradicate any sense of That Other Holiday while we focus in on Hanukah. We all look at Rivka like kindergartners waiting for their teacher to describe the next activity.

Rivka hands me a book of matches. I smile when I see what's printed on it: THE BRIAR PATCH. She has another book in her hands. She looks at me and nods, and I understand that this means I am to do just as she does. She lights the middle candle, which we already know from my crack Internet research is called the shammes, on her beautiful menorah. I do the same on our brand-new shiny store-bought menorah. She extinguishes the lit match with a flick of her wrist. I do the same, but it takes me three flicks to get it to go out. Then she starts to sing again in that soft, low, beautiful voice of hers as she takes the shammes and with its flickering flame lights the remaining six candles. Dad has always had this terrible habit of singing along with anything and everything, even when it's clear he has never heard the song before and doesn't know any of the words, so he starts humming along with Rivka as she sings in Hebrew, but somehow, tonight, this works. There is music in our house, beautiful, soulful, and melancholy music to rival *A Charlie Brown*

Christmas. The candles are all lit, fourteen of them. Their flames are reflected in the mirror above the mantel, so the fourteen become twenty-eight candles burning. Rivka starts to sing again, a different tune, and Dad hums along. I gaze at the candles and their reflection in the mirror, and at my own reflection, and it is as if my face is surrounded by twenty-eight bright and shining stars.

The singing is over. The candles are burning. Rivka goes to the hallway, where she deposited her bags when she arrived, and returns to the living room with her arms full. "Presents."

She gives Mom and Dad a basket with wine, expensive-looking olive oils, jars of preserves, and small tins of spices, which makes Dad practically drool. She hands Jake a package, and he looks a little embarrassed because I'm sure he didn't get her anything, but he still tears greedily into the paper. Rivka knit Jake a striped wool hat with earflaps and a matching scarf. He looks totally adorable when he puts them on; he jumps up and checks himself in the mirror and seems pleased. Then Rivka hands me my present. It's large and flat and square. Unlike Jake, I'm careful and precise when I open my gifts. I always imagine that I could reuse the paper, but of course I never do. This wrapping paper is blue with white stars, and inside I find a gorgeous leather photo album. I run my hands over it.

"This is beautiful. I love it." I start to open it, but Rivka reaches over and gently closes it.

"You might want to wait until later to look at it."

I just assumed it was empty, but now I understand that Rivka has filled it for me, and she understands that I might want to wait for a quieter, more private moment to look at all those people, all that past.

I reach under the tree for Rivka's present and think for a minute that I probably shouldn't have put it under the tree, but she doesn't seem to mind at all. I smile when I hand it to her because of the remarkable symmetry of our gifts. I give Rivka a box filled with picture frames from one of my favorite stores in Boston. In the end I bought seven frames, mostly small ones, in different shapes, each in a weathered painted wood that I figured would go well in her house. She's sitting with the open box on her lap carefully looking at each one, and I notice that her eyes are filling with tears. I can tell that I don't need to explain my gift. She understands that I want her to put her family into these frames and put the frames all around her house. She understands that what I wanted to tell her with this gift was that you can't lock your past in a drawer just because it's too complicated or painful to look at every day.

*　　*　　*

Even before we sit down to dinner, it becomes clear that Rivka is not driving back to the Cape tonight. Not in this snowstorm. No one is going anywhere, so we are in no hurry. We sit around the dinner table until well past ten. Just in case you were wondering, goose is kind of nasty, and unfortunately, although it smells like chicken, it doesn't taste at all like chicken. But Rivka proclaims that the latkes are among the best she's ever had, that they even stand up to Hannah's, which I imagine is quite a compliment. Dad grins proudly. When Jake asks what potato pancakes have to do with Hanukah, Rivka tells the Hanukah story about how there was this oil and it was only supposed to burn for one night but instead it lasted for eight nights, so during Hanukah you should fry stuff in oil. Jake nods as if this makes perfect sense to him.

I spend the evening watching Rivka closely, looking for signs of her illness. Does she seem tired? Is she paler than usual? Does she seem to move more slowly or with more deliberation? Does she have a decreased appetite? (This last question isn't really fair because I wouldn't expect anyone to eat much of Dad's goose.) The problem is, I don't know Rivka well enough to judge when things are changing or slipping. Tonight she seems very much alive. And this fact alone is still a novelty to me.

After dinner Rivka teaches Jake how to play dreidel, and they sit on the floor spinning it and shouting out and exchanging chocolate coins that Rivka supplied. Jake is still wearing his wool hat with the earflaps, and they seem to be having a great time. I sneak upstairs to call Cleo and check how her night with Darius and Jules went. She sounds tired and happy. "He gave me a beautiful necklace. I'm never taking it off."

When did she become this person?

I call James, who says that he's planning on staying up all night waiting by the fireplace so he can hitch a ride out of this hellhole on the fat man's sleigh, and I interpret this to mean that his evening wasn't bad at all, because when James is really depressed he loses his sense of humor.

When it's time to go to bed I offer the futon on the floor in my attic to Rivka. We stay up even later looking through the photo album she gave me, looking at her grandparents and parents and brothers and sisters—my great-grandparents and grandparents and uncles and aunts. This has the surprise effect of sending me into a deep, uncomplicated sleep, and when I wake up Rivka is gone.

seventeen

COMING BACK TO SCHOOL AFTER WINTER BREAK is always hard. It isn't like coming back after the summer, when enough time has gone by that you actually miss school and your classmates and even a teacher or two, and you're tanned and fresh and somehow changed from those three months. No, winter has turned you pale, and you're already behind in your work. There's no starting over. But when I come back to school after winter break, one important thing is different: I have a relationship with Zack Meyers. By relationship I don't mean *relationship*. I mean that I saw him almost every day over break and we talked and we drank coffee. I think we're friends now. We aren't just two people who kind of know each other from school anymore. Cleo's worried. She doesn't want Zack to think of me as a friend. She doesn't want me to become another

Amy Flannigan. She thinks it's time to take the next step. That's why she's forcing me to invite Zack to James's birthday party on Saturday night.

James has always hated his birthday. It comes soon after Christmas and New Year's Eve, and he says that for his entire life it's felt as if everyone is done celebrating by the time his birthday rolls around, including James. But this year it's going to be different. I'm helping to throw him a party at Il Bacio, this really fun Italian restaurant in town with huge portions of not-very-good food. Everyone has to pay his or her own way, but we worked out a deal with the restaurant for twenty bucks a person. We have a reservation for fifteen. It would be sixteen with Zack Meyers.

So. How do I do this? How do I ask Zack if he wants to go to James's party without letting on that I have a massive crush on him? How do I act casual, as if it doesn't matter to me one way or the other, yet still signal that I'm receptive if he was to think of this invitation as a date? What I really need to know is, how do I act more like Cleo?

The first thing I decide is that I have to do this where I'm most comfortable: the Organic Oasis. At school I'm still just this girl on the newspaper staff, someone he knows but not as well as he knows Amy Flannigan. At the Organic Oasis I don't have to order my coffee. Zack fixes it for me without asking. But when I stop by the Oasis after school, I find a pale, overweight girl with a serious case of acne standing behind the counter. So you can tell that I'm not *so* obsessed with Zack that I've carefully tracked his work schedule. When I ask about Zack she just shrugs and asks me if I'm going to have any coffee or what. This means that the Invitation is going to have to happen tomorrow at school. Ugh.

By the way, have I mentioned that Jake has a girl-friend? That's right. My little brother, Jake, has a girlfriend. Things with Sam snowballed at the Snow Ball, and now my brother the freshman is going out with Sam the junior. He spends all his time on the phone with her. I've even seen them kissing outside in the parking lot standing by her car. They're both coming to James's birthday party. So my baby brother has a date for the party that I'm helping to organize.

Cleo is bringing Darius. Obviously. They don't do anything without each other anymore. And Ivy has some new boyfriend who doesn't go to our school and who none of us have met. But not everyone has a date. Let's not forget that this is James's party. The birthday boy is going solo, although I know that he has a secret fantasy that Patrick will show up and surprise him. It's funny because James is the realist. He's my friend who always tells you that you're dreaming, it's never going to happen, you're wasting your time even thinking about it. And yet James told me that he sent Patrick an e-mail with the details about Saturday night and then mentioned casually that it would be great if he could make it. I didn't point out to James that it couldn't have been all that casual if he said that he hoped Patrick could make it to a party that's taking place 180 miles away. I didn't tell James that he's dreaming, that it's never going to happen, that he's wasting his time thinking about it, because that isn't the kind of friend I am.

After dinner I go up to the attic and check my e-mail. I don't check it all that often, so I have a ton of junk mail, mostly consisting of offers to enlarge my penis or shrink my monthly mortgage payment. My favorite penis enlargement e-mail has a subject that reads SMASH DOWN WALLS WITH YOUR GIGANTIC MEMBER. Now, I'm not a man. And I don't have a penis. But I hardly think that smashing down walls would be my primary objective if I did have one.

My computer makes that tinkly sound that means I have an instant message. It's from Cleo.

> So?
> So what?
> Don't play stupid. How'd it
>   go w/Zack?
> It didn't. He wasn't at work

195

>
> this afternoon.
>
> R U telling the truth? Did U
> chicken out?
>
> Unless Zack has turned into
> a chubby girl badly in
> need of a new
> dermatologist, he
> absolutely was not at work
> this afternoon.
>
> U gotta ask him tomorrow.
>
> Yeah, yeah, yeah. Get off my
> back.
>
> Nighty-nite.

I've never been able to stomach that shorthand style of instant messaging. You know, when you replace *you* with *U*, or use a :) to indicate a smile, or the thing I hate the most, the annoying *LOL*. It took me months figure out that *LOL* meant "laughing out loud." At first I thought it meant "lots of love." Then I thought it meant "lord, oh lord."

Now Cleo is already gone, signed off, off to bed, and I sit upstairs in my attic, staring at my blank computer screen, feeling just a little bit lonely.

I lie down on my bed and take out the photo album Rivka gave me. I've looked at all of these pictures so carefully over the past few weeks that I'm almost surprised there's anything left of them. I've been searching these people, these strangers, for signs of myself. There are Hannah's parents, Josiah and Esther, with their dark hats and heavy coats and wool scarves, standing on the sidewalk on what appears to be a beautiful sunny day. There's the small old man whose white beard has grown all the way up his cheeks, stopping just at the dark circles under his eyes, and his flat-faced, angry-looking wife with her hair in a severe bun: Abe and Ruth, Mordechai's father and mother. Rivka was named for her grandmother Ruth, who died only days before Mordechai and Hannah planned to share the news of Hannah's first pregnancy. You will notice that Rivka is named Rivka, not Ruth, but I guess Mordechai and Hannah weren't crazy about the name Ruth, and in Jewish custom you can get away with honoring a dead member of your family by using just the first letter of his or her name. I think about the most recently departed member of our family, my grandmother Gladys. Now I see why they let you cheat by using just the first letter.

My favorite picture in the book is of Rivka with her whole family, minus her youngest brother, Zev, who is prominent in Hannah's bulging belly. Rivka looks to be just about my age, and she told me that this was taken six months before she got pregnant. She's skinny and tall and her knees bend in a little toward each other, and she has the look of a young girl who might bloom into a woman if you were to look away for just a second. It's as if she knows that this change is upon her, and no one else in the picture knows it because they're all looking somewhere else or at each other. Only Rivka is looking directly into the camera, like she's letting you in on a secret. But it didn't quite happen that way, did it? She didn't just bloom from a girl into a woman. Rivka's transformation was interrupted by the terrifying surprise of her pregnancy. But then again, maybe that's the secret she's sharing with the camera. Maybe her secret was what was yet to come. Maybe her secret was me.

I figure my best and probably only chance to talk to Zack and extend the Invitation is after our *Gazette* meeting today. I can't concentrate on anything all day long. I don't eat any lunch, I go to the wrong room for fifth period, and I bite my cuticles to the quick. Then I walk into the *Gazette* meeting and learn that Amy Flannigan couldn't make it today, and I take this as some kind of sign. Maybe the stars are lining up for me. Maybe this is my chance. My opportunity. Maybe this is what I need, just a minute alone with Zack after our meeting to turn the tables, to get a new start, to change our destiny. Okay, perhaps I'm taking this a little too far, but I do feel strangely emboldened by Amy's absence. I sit through the meeting and imagine him picking me up before the dinner on Saturday and holding my hand at the table, and I even imagine him kissing me goodnight parked in his car idling in front of my house. And then Zack says sorry, he really wishes he could, but he can't make it on Saturday night.

The conversation went like this.

Me: "Hey, Zack, I was just wondering, if you aren't doing anything on Saturday night, I'm helping throw this party at Il Bacio for my friend James's birthday, and it should be kind of fun, even though the food isn't all that memorable, but there will be a bunch of people there, and if you want to, you could join us."

That was really, really lame, I know.

Him: "That sounds great . . ."

Big goofy smile from me here that despite my best efforts and Cleo's voice echoing in my head I still can't seem to control.

Him: ". . . but I can't make it. I really wish I could, but I'm going to be out of town. I'm visiting my brother at college."

Me: "Oh, well. Next time."

Him: "You mean James's next birthday?"

Me, laughing: "If you think you're getting invited to James's next birthday, you're crazy."

Him: "So what's the next time?"

Me: "That's just something people say when they're trying to be polite."

Him, shrugging: "Oh. I really am sorry that I can't be there. You may think the food isn't memorable, but I daydream about their eggplant parmesan."

This is when it starts to hit me that I've just asked out a boy for the very first time in my life and been rejected.

Me: "Well, I'll see you around."

I walk quickly out of the *Gazette* offices and off the school campus, and I retreat back home.

On the night of the party I get depressed. You know why, right? Because everyone has someone and I'm all alone. Poor me. I'm up in my attic trying to figure out what I should wear and then I realize that it doesn't matter because no one is looking at me anyway. It feels like everyone I know has someone to dress up for, someone to call and make a plan for how to get to the restaurant tonight, someone to ride over in the car with complaining that there's never anything good to listen to on the radio. Sam is picking up Jake. Darius is picking up Cleo. I don't want to go alone. So I call James. He says he'd love it if I would pick him up but that I should make sure to leave enough time to come in the house so his father can take a picture of me pinning on his corsage.

I call the restaurant one more time to confirm our reservation and tell them that we will be fifteen, not sixteen. I go downstairs and find Mom and Dad on the couch reading. Her feet are in his lap, and he is absentmindedly tugging at each of her toes.

Dad looks up from his book. "You look beautiful tonight, sweetheart."

All I'm wearing are jeans, black boots, and a long-sleeved brown T-shirt. But I did get a new lipstick from Rivka after I told her about ten times that I loved the color on her, and tonight is the first time I've worn it. I know he's my dad and that this is what dads say to their daughters, especially when they use their dad powers to pick up on the fact that their daughters are feeling particularly vulnerable, but it's nice to hear that I look beautiful to someone. Even if it is just my dad.

"So what are you two party animals doing tonight?" I ask.

Mom looks at Dad, and they both shrug. "I don't know. Eat a little something. Maybe watch a movie," she says. They smile at each other. They look like they could sit this way on the couch all night, with her feet in his lap, without getting up, and that it would be a completely perfect evening.

"So Sam and Jake are going to the dinner . . . ," Dad says.

Of course Sam and Jake are going to the dinner. Mom and Dad know that already. I suspect that Dad is hoping that by just mentioning Sam he can draw from me some kind of comment about Sam and Jake and their new relationship, but I'm not biting. He should know better. I'm not going to talk about Jake's personal life with them, and I would hope that if I had a personal life, Jake wouldn't talk about mine with Mom and Dad. I don't really know Sam. I feel a little awkward around her because she's in my class and she's dating my little brother, but she seems perfectly nice and Jake seems really happy (although, honestly, I can't remember a time when Jake didn't seem really happy), and even though I feel lonely tonight, I think it's great that they found each other. But all I say to Mom and Dad is "I'm off to get the birthday boy," and I kiss them both good night.

When I get to James's house I call him from my cell phone because I think it's rude to honk and I don't like his parents because they made him feel so terrible when he finally got up the courage to come out to them, which I know was the hardest thing he ever had to do, so I want him to meet me outside. He tells me to come in, that he isn't quite ready, and that no one else is home.

I find him in his room, just out of the shower, standing in front of the mirror in a pair of black jeans. I know he's been working out after school, but he looks as scrawny as he ever did.

"I have nothing to wear," he says.

"Well, lucky for you, today is your birthday," I say, and hand him his gift.

It's a PROM QUEEN T-shirt, the same one I made for Cleo, except it isn't made out of the clingy material that is flattering on a girl with boobs like hers. It is loose-fitting, in dark blue with gold letters.

"You know I always wanted that shirt," James says, and he quickly throws on a white long-sleeved thermal and then puts the T-shirt over it. He smiles at himself in the mirror and then turns around to me with his arms outstretched. At first I think he's saying, *Look at me*, but then I realize he's waiting for me to hug him.

"Happy birthday," I say as I give him a squeeze. "Let's go to your party."

He links his arm through mine, and we go downstairs and out of the house and into my still-warm car and head off to Il Bacio.

The party is great. They gave us a private room with a painted mural on the ceiling, and we sit at one long table with a red and white checked tablecloth and candles burning in old Chianti bottles. James sits in a chair that looks like a throne. I watch Jake and Sam all through dinner, and he's so considerate and polite, making sure she has everything she needs and involving her in all his conversations. Sam may be two years older than Jake, but she's shy and quiet and seems a little unsure of herself. She wears the striped wool hat with the earflaps that Rivka knit for Jake, and his arm is draped over the back of her chair. Even though I'm sure Jake would hate for me to describe them this way, they just look so *cute* together.

And then right before the waiter brings out the birthday cake—a carrot cake, per James's request, which seems like a complete waste of cake to me—something extraordinary happens. A true birthday miracle. Let's just say that I would have been dead wrong if I had said to James that he was dreaming, that it was never going to happen, that he was wasting his time just thinking about it.

That's right. Patrick walks through the door.

I've never met Patrick, but I know the minute I see James's face that the blond guy standing in the doorway with the black-framed glasses and green leather jacket is the boy for whom James has been pining since the summer. James jumps up and they hold each other for a really long time, and everyone else continues on with their conversations, trying to create the illusion that James and Patrick are having a private moment. Then James asks the waiter for an extra chair, another place is set at the table—the sixteenth place, which I was hoping would be for Zack—and James introduces Patrick proudly to all of his friends.

Somehow, even though I've been moping around all afternoon and evening and even though tonight James was supposed to be my date, my partner in isolation, the surprise of Patrick showing up and the sight of James sitting with him snap me out of my mood. I can't wipe the smile from my face. My heart is singing. Even the carrot cake is delicious. And then James gets a ride home with Patrick, and I leave the party happy and alone.

eighteen

RIVKA HAS AN APPOINTMENT at Beth Israel Hospital in Boston and calls to see if I want to meet her in the city for dinner. That doesn't sound good, does it? Driving all the way from the Cape for an appointment at the hospital can't be a sign that things are going well. I ask her how she's feeling, which is the closest I've come to actually acknowledging that she's sick, and she says okay, but she says okay in the way that really means *I feel like crap.* So we make plans to meet at Pho Pasteur, which is probably my favorite restaurant in Boston, and Mom and Dad don't seem to mind that I'm taking the car into the city alone and won't be home until hours after it gets dark.

When I get there Rivka is waiting, drinking an avocado milk shake. I laugh because I'm the only person I know who likes the Pho Pasteur avocado milk shake—everyone always makes a face when I order it, which is something I do without fail every time I eat at Pho Pasteur. It's a perfect night for pho, the specialty of the house, a big steaming bowl of Vietnamese noodle soup. It's sleeting outside. It isn't quite cold enough for snow, but it's too cold for rain. And yet, even in this weather, Mom and Dad let me take the car into the city.

I slide into the booth across from her. She smiles at me. I look at her face and recognize that this is not a real smile. This is a smile like her okay was an okay. Her eyes look worried and sad.

"Tell me," I say, "how did it go today?"

"Honestly?"

"Sure."

"Not so hot."

I feel a tightening in my stomach, a shortness of breath, a wave of heat on this icy evening. Panic. Rivka is here to tell me that she's dying. No, wait. I already knew that. She already told me that she's dying, but I guess I haven't accepted that this is really going to happen. That this isn't just something to talk about and then wait for it to go away. That this isn't just a brief chapter in my impossible life.

Something is terribly wrong with Rivka, and I can't keep pretending that she's fine.

I take a sip of my milk shake. The avocado tastes a little off.

"I had to come in for some testing to follow up on something I had done last week, and honestly, I am tired of testing and follow-ups to follow-up testing because I'm not testing so well these days."

"What do the doctors say?"

"They say I should eat. Let's order dinner."

I've lost my appetite, but I order a bowl of pho anyway. My dad always talks about the restorative properties of pho. If you feel the first hints of a cold, eat a bowl of pho and you'll avoid the flu. If you feel achy, eat a bowl of pho and the fever that was creeping up on you will beat a quick retreat. But tonight I don't think this pho can cure what's ailing me. And we know that Rivka needs something much, much stronger than a bowl of noodle soup with secret spices.

Rivka orders the lemongrass tofu, and when it arrives she seems to spend more time moving the tofu around on her plate with her chopsticks than she does moving the food into her mouth.

"I'm sorry to be such a downer tonight, Simone. I didn't ask you here to burden you with all of this." She puts her chopsticks down and picks up a fork and uses the fork to move her tofu around the plate. "I asked you here because right now I enjoy your company more than the company of anyone else in the whole world. So tell me something. Tell me a couple of things. Tell me some stories to remember on my long drive home tonight. Tell me the best thing that happened to you this week. And then tell me the crappiest thing."

"Well," I say, "it looks like the ACLU has won its town seal case." I go on to explain the case and how after a pretrial hearing the town just caved because they decided that it wasn't worth the time or the money to fight a case they probably couldn't win.

And then to my total shock Rivka tells me, "I'm glad it never made it to trial. I think a case like that is a complete waste of the ACLU's time."

"That's like slapping me in the face!" I say. "I fought hard for this. I spent a precious Saturday gathering signatures. I rallied at the town hall. I squared off against a villain more frightening than you could possibly imagine." I tell her all about the Evil Bitch and her Towering Kingdom of Self-Righteousness. Rivka laughs.

"And you of all people," I say. "I just can't understand how you don't see a cross on a town seal as a worthy cause."

"I just think there are far more important causes to fight for. There are people who live in fear. In abject poverty. There are people who need lawyers as a matter of life and death. There are liberties and freedoms that are getting trampled and kicked and pummeled for sport in the world today, and we need every ounce of fight the ACLU has left in it. A cross on a town seal is symbolic. It's cosmetic. It doesn't have any truly debilitating effect on anyone."

"I respect your point of view, but I totally disagree. I think you have to keep a sharp eye on the little things before they become the big things."

Rivka smiles at me. "Your mother must be so proud of you. And you must be so proud of her."

"Yeah, I guess I am. But she's entirely useless in the field of the crappiest thing that happened to me this week."

"What field is that?"

"Boys. I can't even talk to her about that stuff because all she ever says is something about how great I am and how anyone would be lucky to date me and blah blah blah."

"So what happened?"

"I asked Zack out and he said, 'No way, not in a million years, you repel me.'"

"He said 'No way, not in a million years, you repel me'?"

"He said something like 'That sounds great, I wish I could, but I can't,' which to me is the same as 'No way, not in a million years, you repel me.'"

The waiter is hovering around our table, not sure if he can clear two meals that haven't been eaten. Rivka has perked up a bit. Some color has returned to her face, and although she has barely touched her tofu, she's on her second milk shake. I wonder what all this bad testing means. What comes next? What do they do when your tests are bad? Get you a tutor? No. They do drastic things that make you sick and weak and make you lose your hair. So Rivka may wind up in a wig after all, which is how I imagined her before she walked through my door on Thanksgiving after-noon—in a wig and not nearly as beautiful.

"Are you going to have to get chemo?"

"I've already had chemo. It obviously didn't work, although I guess that isn't the right way to look at it. It did work for a while. But now I'm beyond it. The doctors say I could try it again, but it isn't likely to do much other than make me feel terrible."

I feel tears coming on, but I also know that this isn't what Rivka needs right now.

"This is just so unfair."

Rivka laughs.

"What's so funny?"

"Oh, I don't know. Nothing, really. It's just that I used to get hung up on thinking about fairness and why and why me and why now. And it just doesn't get you anywhere. It's like those questions you used to pester your parents with. Why? Why? Why? Finally they get fed up and say, 'Just because.' And that's the only real answer here. Just because."

I'm having a thought. An idea. It's gnawing away at me, and even though I have a sense that this isn't something I should say out loud, somehow with Rivka I feel like I can say anything at all.

"Do you ever think God is punishing you? Do you ever think that maybe if you hadn't turned your back on your faith this wouldn't be happening?"

Rivka takes a deep breath, and for a minute I think I've offended her, but then I see that she's just carefully considering her answer.

"Simone. First of all, I didn't turn my back on my faith. It's important to me that you understand this. I left the Hasidic community that raised me to find my own way and to discover my own relationship to Judaism, a relationship that I believe is every bit as valid. And here's what I think about God. I think God exists in moments of grace and beauty and good fortune. I think things like this, like my sickness, are just bad, bad luck. Things like this happen just because."

This strikes me as a pretty generous interpretation of God. How can she let Him off the hook so easily? Why does He only get credit for the good stuff? I want to argue this out with her, but I don't think tonight's the night.

"Do *they* know?" I ask.

"My family?"

"Yes."

"No. They don't."

"Why not?"

"Because I want them to see me for who I am, to accept my choices and my life because this is what's right for me, not because they're worried that they'll feel guilty for not accepting me when it's too late. I don't want acceptance or forgiveness or whatever it is I need from them to come out of pity or out of a sense that this is their last chance."

"Huh."

"What?"

"I guess I just don't see what's wrong with letting people know that it's their last chance to make something right."

She stares at me for a long time without saying a word.

"How old are you again?"

"Officially, sixteen."

Rivka shakes her head. She reaches across the table and squeezes my hand. I squeeze hers back.

"How's Cleo doing?"

"Same. Obsessing about her boyfriend, who I still suspect is an imposter, a villain masquerading as Prince Charming."

"Rule number one: always beware a Prince

Charming." She makes a loud slurping noise as she reaches the bottom of her second milk shake. For a brief moment she looks like a little girl.

"Is there anything I can do?" I ask.

"You're already doing it," she says.

Rivka walks me to my car. We're both carrying to-go bags heavy with our uneaten dinners. We walk through the streets of a student neighborhood. Considering Boston has 250,000 students living here, to a certain extent every neighborhood is a student neighborhood, but the students are packed with particular density in this part of town, the location of the Pho Pasteur we ate in without eating in tonight. It has warmed up a little, the skies have cleared, and the sidewalks are wet but not icy. There's a long line outside what must be some kind of nightclub. Huddles of students stand in heavy coats and wool hats, smoking cigarettes, talking and laughing too loudly. Life just looks so easy for these college kids. I realize that all of this is waiting for me not too far down the road. I'm staring at my future (minus the cigarettes). And seeing this all before me, I feel strangely guilty.

When I get back home my parents are sitting on the couch, Mom looking through some files and Dad reading the newspaper. Either they're getting good at pretending they don't worry about me out on the road by myself at night or else they're getting used to the idea. I ask about Jake, and Dad gives me a look that means *Do you even have to ask?* and this is how I know that Jake is in his room on the phone with Sam. I sit down in the armchair facing them and pull off my boots. My big toe is sticking out of a hole in my sock, and I stare at it. "She's really sick," I say.

"Yes, honey, we know." Mom looks at me and then at Dad.

I start to cry, and they just let me. They don't rush over to hold me or stroke my hair or wipe the tears from my face or tell me that it's going to be okay, and I appreciate this tremendously.

"It just makes me so sad to think of her all alone. No one should live life like that. No one should live alone and no one should have to die alone."

"Oh, I don't think she's alone. She has friends. Lots of friends who are like family to her. And now she has you," says Mom.

"It's just so ironic." I wipe my running nose on my sleeve.

Dad looks at me. "What's ironic?"

"Well, she gave me up because she was afraid that her family and community would reject her if she had a baby. Then she ended up leaving them all anyway. So in the end she could have kept me and then at least she would have had a daughter. And she wouldn't be alone right now."

"True," says Mom. "But then *you* would have been left alone, and I think that would have been unbearable for her. It would have made this even harder on her than it is already."

I press my fingers into my eyes until I become dizzy with the bright colors and shapes swirling in front of me.

"This is too much. It makes my head hurt. I think I just need to get some sleep."

I say good night and go over to the stairs.

"Oh, wait. Simone?" Mom calls from the living room.

I come back in. "Yeah?"

"You have a message," she says, and hands me a scrap of paper on which she has written in her annoyingly perfect penmanship: *Zack called. He said he wants to talk about the next time*.

nineteen

NATURALLY, THE FIRST THING I DO is call Cleo. It's too late to call Zack. It's too late to call Cleo, but this is an emergency. I read her the message. She says she doesn't get it, and then I remind her of my exchange with him, which I had told her word for word. Cleo says, "Oh, my God. He was totally calling to ask you out." And then I tell her about my dinner with Rivka, and she says, "What a night you're having."

We hang up, and I spend what's left of the night tossing and turning and not getting one minute of sleep. I'm sad about Rivka. I'm excited about Zack. I don't know which emotion to stick with—they keep crashing into each other all night long.

So, as you can imagine, I'm not looking my best in the morning. The day goes by in a blur, and I don't mean it goes by quickly. It's painfully slow. Nothing is in focus for me except the conversation that hasn't taken place yet. I run through several variations, including one where I completely misunderstand the meaning of his message and make a total fool out of myself.

Cleo had Spanish class with Zack third period. At lunch she confirms that he's here today, and then she swears that she didn't say a thing to him and that she didn't give him any kind of knowing or teasing look, and I have no choice but to believe her. James has abandoned his usual role of the skeptic and gets all gushy and excited for me because this is the new James. The post-Patrick's-surprise-visit James is an undying romantic.

When the final bell rings and I head for the *Gazette* office, my heart is pounding so loudly in my chest that I'm certain everyone walking by me in the hallway can hear it. I imagine that everyone is staring at me, knowing that I'm on my way to see what this message from Zack is all about. As you can see, the night of no sleep has left me a bit delirious.

And there he is, with a pencil behind his ear, sitting with his camouflage-high-topped feet up on the conference table. He doesn't see me come in. He's talking with Amy Flannigan and Marcel. I take a seat at the far end of the table, which is quickly filling up with the other staffers. Someone drops a book on the floor, and Zack looks up. Our eyes meet, and he gives me the sweetest smile and then a little wave with his fingers. I start to mouth that I'm sorry I didn't call him back, but his look says, *What are you talking about?* I hold up my hand to my ear to indicate a telephone. He gives a nod and a wave as if to say, *Don't worry about it.*

Marcel starts the meeting.

I get assigned a profile of two Russian exchange students. Or maybe it's about two students who are going on an exchange program to Russia. I'm not really paying attention. The meeting finally wraps up, and everyone is hanging around chatting. I take a long time to pack up my notebook because Zack is still talking to Amy and Marcel, and I wait for a few minutes, but then I start to feel pathetic, so I throw my backpack over my shoulder and leave.

Zack comes after me in the hall.

"Wait up."

"Sorry. It looked like you were in the middle of something. Anyway," I say, "I just wanted to apologize for not calling you back last night. I didn't get home until late."

Oh, God. He's wearing this gray sweater, and it makes his eyes look amazing, and I think it would feel really soft to the touch, but don't worry—I have enough of a grip on things to know that I need to keep my hands to myself.

"That's okay. I just wanted to know how James's birthday party was."

That's it? That's all he wanted to know? He just wanted to know about James's birthday party? I'm such a fool. Why did I have to call Cleo? Why did I have to talk about it with James over lunch? Why did I have to make such a big deal out of one phone call? One stupid message?

"It was great."

"Did you have the eggplant parmesan?"

"No. I had the linguini with mushrooms. Sorry."

"You mean linguini con funghi?"

"I thought you took Spanish."

"I do. But I also dabble in Italian." He shifts his weight and looks past me down the hallway. Then he looks the other way. Is he waiting for someone? He looks back at me. "So what do you think about trying out the eggplant parmesan this Saturday night?"

Here comes that huge grin of mine again. I can't stop it. I actually put my hands up and cover my heart as if I have to hold it there, as if it might jump right out of my chest.

"I'd love to."

"Good."

He smiles, and I smile back. In fact, I smile all the way home.

I have a date with Zack. I have a date. With Zack.

Me. Simone. Simone has a date with Zack. This Saturday night for eggplant parmesan. At Il Bacio. Okay. Please remember something. Remember that this has never happened to me before. Remember that I've only kissed three boys, one during a stupid game and the other two at parties involving alcohol, and I puked after the most recent of these experiences. I've never stood face to face with a boy in the full light of day (or, more accurately, in the full fluorescent light of the school hallway) and had a conversation in which it becomes obvious that we both really like each other. I'm sixteen years and nine months old and I've never been asked on a date. I've never gone on a date. Now do you understand why I'm acting like such a freak?

I get home from school and call Cleo and James. Then I call Rivka.

"See?" she says. "I told you, you don't repel him."

"Is this your version of 'Any boy would be lucky to date you, blah blah blah'?"

"I suppose it is. So, what are you going to wear?"

"I can't even think about it yet. All I know is that I'm definitely going to wear that lipstick you gave me."

"Good call."

"So I'll give you a ring Sunday morning. After the big night."

There's a pause.

"I won't be here, Simone. I have to check into Beth Israel tomorrow for a few days. I won't get out until Monday. But you can reach me there."

"I can call you there?"

"Of course you can. It isn't jail. It's just the hospital for more testing."

"You have to spend the weekend in the hospital?"

"Yeah. It's okay, though. They have cable, unlike my backwoods house."

"Can I come visit?"

"It sounds like you have a lot going on this weekend already."

"Not tomorrow night. I'll bring dinner. Can you eat?"

"I can try."

Once again, as you can probably imagine, Mom and Dad put up no resistance to my taking the car into the city on Friday night. Dad even spends the afternoon making dinner for Rivka and me, which he packs in a picnic basket with real plates and silverware. Roast chicken with rosemary sweet potatoes and creamed spinach. I call this bakery I love that's halfway between here and the city to find out if they make challah. They do. I ask them to hold two for me. I take some candles and two small candlesticks, and I coax Dad into letting me bring a bottle of wine. I figure that being in the hospital doesn't mean Rivka should have to miss out on Shabbat.

All the traffic is moving in the opposite direction. This makes no sense to me. I don't understand why people want to get out of the city. If I had my choice, I'd spend not just my weekends but my whole life in the city. Why would you go away from the place with all the action and vitality on the few days of the week when you actually have time to enjoy all the action and vitality? There must be some good answer, because all roads leading out of Boston are bumper-to-bumper, and I'm flying in toward the city center.

I park in the underground maze of the parking lot. Purple level. Section C. As I grab the picnic basket and put on my sweatshirt, I feel like Little Red Riding Hood skipping off into the woods, except unlike Little Red, I know the danger that lurks in the forest.

It isn't as bad as I imagined. She has an IV in and a few of those round plastic things on her chest connecting her through wires to some kind of machine, but it beeps in a calm and not terribly urgent manner. *Beep . . . beep . . . beep.* There are no tubes in her nose. Nothing over her mouth. She has her bed propped up, and she's watching television.

She smiles when I walk in, and shuts off the TV.

"Thank God you're here. I was about to get sucked into this idiotic reality show. I don't know if I could have lived with myself if I'd seen it through the whole hour."

"Glad I could be of service," I say. I hold up the picnic basket. "Hungry?"

I wheel the end table over from the other side of the bed and spread out our dinner. I ask the nurse if she can score us another table, and she brings in a tray on wheels. On this I place the candles and the challah, and I open the wine and fill a plastic cup with it.

"Oooh. Contraband," says Rivka.

"The wine or the candles?"

"Both, I'm sure. But I don't think anyone will give us a hard time. It's one of the benefits of terminal illness. You can get away with anything."

Terminal. The word echoes in my head. It lodges in my throat. It clamps itself around my heart. *Terminal: fatal, deadly, incurable.*

I take one of the cloth napkins Dad packed and use it to cover the challah. I hand Rivka a book of matches. She grabs my hand and then strokes my arm.

"This is wonderful. Thank you."

She tries to light the match, but the IV seems to be giving her some trouble, so I take care of it. I take a pitcher of water and help her wash her hands. We do the blessings over the candles and then the wine and the bread. I move closer and she puts her hands on my head, her hands with their trailing wires, and she says a blessing over me even though I don't really think I'm the one in need of prayer right now.

I remember her house and how warm and cozy it was on Shabbat. I remember how the candles illuminated the room. The sound of the wind in the trees. The smell of the sea. Things couldn't be more different here tonight. The room is an unpleasant lime green. The lights are too bright. The sounds are of machines and carts being wheeled down the halls and muffled conversations behind closed doors. The smell is antiseptic. But you would never know that anything was different if you looked only at Rivka's face. She wears the same blissful look she wore when we celebrated Shabbat at her home.

I'm happy to see that she eats heartily. We talk and we laugh, and for brief interludes I manage to forget where we are and why. It starts to get late, and she's tired and I have to make the drive home, so I pack up my basket and dump the rest of the wine (that was part of the deal I struck with Dad). I say good night to Rivka and find my way back to purple level, section C, and I go home.

*   *   *

On Saturday I have my scheduled wardrobe consultation with Cleo two hours before Zack is due to pick me up. She comes over with a suitcase of clothes. I guess this shows what kind of faith she has in my closet. We settle on a pair of jeans with a gray scoop-neck shirt of Cleo's with the Cleo signature cling and a long black cardigan sweater with a belt that Cleo firmly tells me I am *not* to tie shut. I wear black shoes with a very small heel because I've taken notice that Zack has only about two inches on me. I wear the lipstick Rivka gave me.

"I can't believe little Simone is all grown up and going on a date," Cleo says as she studies her handiwork.

"It must be strange for you to conceive of a date that takes place *before* the two parties have been naked in bed together."

"That's low."

"Oh, come on. Have a sense of humor."

"You're just lucky that I'm in a charitable mood. Darius invited me to go skiing with his family over spring break, and believe it or not, Jules said I could go."

"That's great, Cleo."

She adjusts the belt on the sweater. She takes my hair in her hands. "Hold still." She pulls it up and considers what I would look like with it in a ponytail, then she thinks better of it and lets it go.

"Well," she says, "you look perfect. My work here is done." She gives me a hug and takes her suitcase home.

Zack arrives right on time. I answer the door and let him into the entryway just long enough to grab my scarf and my purse, and then we're off. I couldn't stand a whole come-on-in-and-be-inspected-by-the-parents scene, so Mom and Dad agree to stay in the kitchen. They take me at my word that Zack is a nice boy from school, not some old pervert or deranged coke addict I met at the mall.

The drive over to Il Bacio helps calm my nerves; it gives us a chance to talk without having to make eye contact. It gives me a chance to study his profile and take in exactly how adorable he looks tonight without him reading this all over my face. He's wearing a brown suede jacket and a light green V-neck sweater. He's freshly shaven. His hair still looks a little wet, and he smells like hair product. To top it off, he has *A Rush of Blood to the Head* playing on the car stereo. Could he be any more perfect?

Our table is in the back, in a little corner by a fireplace that is filled with burning candles rather than logs, and I'm grateful because, as I think I've mentioned, I tend to sweat when I'm nervous. The waiter brings our menus and fills our water glasses, and then Zack folds his arms on the table and takes a long look at me.

"Hi," he says.

I'm not sure why, but this just completely disarms me. He looks so comfortable and so happy to be here, like he wants to savor every minute. I know how he feels. I'm feeling the exact same way.

"Zack," I say, "there's something I have to tell you."

That look of comfort is replaced by a look of concern.

"What is it?"

"This isn't easy for me," I say. I pause and take a sip of my water. "I can't stand eggplant."

The dinner is amazing. I don't mean the food. I stand by my earlier proclamation that the food isn't very memorable. But the evening is magical. I can hardly believe that I'm here, that this is happening, that life can be so perfect and so uncomplicated.

After they clear our plates and before they bring the dessert, Zack looks at me and says, "You probably already knew this, but I've had a mad crush on you since you came in for coffee that morning when you were gathering signatures for the ACLU."

"Really?"

"Yeah. There's nothing hotter than a chick who

gets up early in the morning to fight for the underdog."

I'm blushing. He takes my hand. Now I'm really blushing.

"And," he says, "you look so cute first thing in the morning."

"You didn't look half bad yourself. I like you in an apron."

He laughs. "This is really nice."

"Yeah. It is."

The waiter brings the tiramisu. Neither of us even looks at it.

"Do you know what Il Bacio means in Italian?" he asks.

"No. I'm helpless with foreign languages. I'm barely passing remedial French."

"It means 'the kiss.'"

I sit there speechless.

"Now I bet you're thinking that I'm going to use this as a segue into how amazing you look tonight and how all I can think about is how much I want to kiss you and since the name of this restaurant actually means 'the kiss,' there really is no reasonable alternative."

Still can't get my brain to construct anything approaching an intelligent sentence.

"So, what do you think? I mean, I hate to be so

predictable, but this is exactly why I brought up the whole Il Bacio thing." I smile and nod. Yes. I think yes.

He gets up and leans over the table, over the tiramisu, and he takes my face in his hands and he gives me the sweetest, most gentle, most delicious, most wonderful, most perfect kiss.

twenty

BEFORE I WAKE UP, before I get the chance to let last night come back to me, before I can lie here in my bed remembering every detail of my date with Zack, I hear his voice.

"Hi."

I check my clock. Five minutes past ten.

"Hi," I say.

"Did I call too early? You sound sleepy."

"No, no. I'm up."

"Liar."

"Okay. So I lied. I promise I won't lie to you ever again."

"What are you doing?"

"Didn't I just admit that I was sleeping?"

"Want to take a walk?"

"Sure. Is there coffee somewhere on this walk?"

"I think we can make that happen. I'll see you in

half an hour?"

"Great."

This must be it. This must be when he comes over and tells me that I'm really great and I'm a good friend but that he's made some kind of terrible mistake and he's sorry but he doesn't have *those* kinds of feelings for me and can we just be friends? And by the way, he's in love with Amy Flannigan.

This time, because I don't have a choice in the matter, I invite him in and introduce him to my parents. They stand there, Dad's arm around Mom's waist, beaming at him. "It's so nice to meet you and we've heard so much about you," they say. It isn't even eleven o'clock and this is the second lie of the day. Mom and Dad haven't heard so much about Zack. All I told them was that bit about him not being a pervert or a cocaine addict. They don't know about my long-simmering crush on him. They don't know that I asked him to James's party or that we sat in his car kissing for almost an hour last night. They don't know that he's about to dump me. But they stand there smiling at him like they've been waiting for this moment all their lives.

It's cold out. There's snow on the ground, but the sky is bright blue. The sunlight bouncing off the white of the snow is blinding. My fingers are numb even though I'm wearing fleece gloves. I want to reach for his hand, to warm my fingers in his, but I know that I can't. We walk in silence for what feels like an eternity. I can't stand it anymore. Why is he so quiet? We had so much to say to each other in the candlelight of Il Bacio last night, but this morning the startlingly bright sunlight is somehow creating a void between us. And what do I do? I fill it. I start to ramble. I'm talking a mile a minute. I'm telling him all about Rivka. I'm telling him all about me and my life and how I knew about her but I didn't really want to know about her so I worked hard never to think about her and then one day I called her and now she's a part of my life and now I'm losing her. I'm losing her again.

I tell him about Mordechai, but he stops me and tells me that he already knows the story of Mordechai. That's right. I forgot about the article I wrote about Mom for the *Gazette*. About her first case. About the Hasidic family in the little community south of Boston. He took the pictures of Mom for that story.

"That is where you come from? Rivka is Mordechai's daughter?"

I nod.

"Wow. That's amazing."

He takes my hand and smiles at me. My fingers begin to regain their feeling.

We stop at a café in town that I've never been to. Zack says, "The coffee here is much better than at the Organic Oasis. Our coffee may be fair trade, but that doesn't keep it from tasting like metal."

He pulls off my gloves and rubs my cold hands in his.

"That's how I knew you liked me. Why else would anyone drink that coffee?"

My hands are warming up, and so is the rest of me. I didn't imagine last night. It was real. Zack is real. What is happening between us is really happening.

He goes to the counter to order while I find a table. He returns with two plain no-frills coffees and a chocolate croissant, which he places on the table between us.

I smile weakly at him.

"You look sad," he says.

"I'm not. I mean I am. I mean, I'm really happy right now. I love this café, and that croissant looks great, and I don't understand why you didn't get one for yourself. But I also can't stop thinking about Rivka sitting all alone in Beth Israel Hospital."

"Let's go see her."

"Really?"

"Absolutely."

We transfer our coffees into to-go cups and walk back to my house and tell my parents where we're going.

We say a quick hi to Jake, who has finally emerged from his room, and we get in Zack's car and head for the city.

When we arrive Rivka has three visitors: two women and a man with long hair, who I mistake for a third woman when we first enter. Rivka seems delighted that I've stopped by, even though I feel like I just crashed a party. The hellos are a little strange because these friends obviously know who I am even though we've never met, and Rivka obviously knows who Zack is, so there are a lot of hands being shaken and pretending not to know the person whose hand is being shaken. Rivka's friends stay for a few more minutes and then start talking about how they have to make the drive back to the Cape, and wow, look at the time. One of the women makes arrangements to pick up Rivka tomorrow, and this makes me feel a little bit better. They leave, and it's just Rivka and Zack and me and the calm beeping of the hospital machinery.

"So," Rivka says, "I guess the date went well last night."

You'd think this would embarrass me, but now that I'm pretty sure Zack isn't planning on telling me that last night was a big mistake, it doesn't embarrass me at all.

"Exceptionally well," he says, and shoots me a grin.

"How are you feeling?" I ask.

"Tired of this place. Tired of lying in bed. Tired of cable TV."

"They liberate you tomorrow?"

"Amen. Lila is picking me up." Rivka readjusts her pillows and props herself up. "And on our way back home I'm stopping off to see my family because someone I know who is very wise advised me to give them one last chance."

We stay for about an hour. Zack talks to Rivka about the Red Sox (I had no idea she was a baseball fan), about Cape Cod, and about photography. He says that he's never had enough faith in himself to shoot landscapes. He's always searching for a definable subject. Rivka says she knows exactly what he means (that makes one of us) but that she always had the opposite problem. She never had enough faith that the meaning of her subjects was comprehensible to anyone but her, and that's why she works in the more neutral and ambiguous realm of landscape. I just sit in my uncomfortable plastic chair and watch them go back and forth. I remember thinking that maybe I could be a photographer. Clearly I was wrong.

When we get up to leave, Zack says goodbye and waits for me in the hall. I give Rivka a hug, and she whispers in my ear, "He's perfect," and I feel my eyes welling up with tears.

"What happened to rule number one: beware a Prince Charming?"

"I guess rules are made to be broken."

I pull the sheet up and tuck her in. I kiss her forehead.

When we step into the elevator Zack puts his arms around me and takes his thumb and wipes a tear from my cheek.

Going back to school is strange because it feels as if my whole life has changed in this one weekend. But in other ways, everything is just the same. I'm running through my SAT vocabulary words, struggling in French class, sailing through calculus, and gossiping with my friends at lunch.

"So tell me," says James, "how was your date with Flash Gordon?"

"We've been through this, James. If you insist on making fun of him, at the very least let him be Harry Potter, boy wizard, rather than some second-rate, steroid-using superhero with totally forgettable powers."

"Okay, okay. Sorry. So?"

"It was awesome. It was perfect. We saw each other on Sunday too."

"Wow. Things seem to be moving right along."

"Yeah, but I'm not sure what to do next. I don't think I'm very good at this."

"Don't think too much about it. Just let it happen."

James's advice would be much easier to take if I'd seen or talked to Zack on Monday. Or Tuesday. Then Wednesday came, and at the *Gazette* meeting he sat next to Amy instead of me. We talked for a while afterward, but I couldn't help feeling hurt that he chose to sit with her when the empty seat by my side was just as available, and it even had armrests!

What's wrong with me? I'm in perfect health. I have a loving (and sometimes annoying) mother and father who accept me for who I am. I have a brother who worships me even though it is indisputable that he is a hundred times cooler than I am. I wake up every morning and drink my juice without the burden of swallowing dozens of different pills, knowing that I have more mornings like this ahead of me than I can possibly fathom. And I just had a great date with a really cute guy only days ago. Why am I spending all this time brooding over how much attention Zack is or isn't paying to me when Rivka is dying alone?

Cleo says I shouldn't be so hard on myself.

"Of course you're worried about whether or not

Zack still likes you. You can worry about Zack at the same time as you worry about Rivka, and that's okay."

"Are you sure about that?"

"Positive. And anyway, Zack is a guy. This is just how guys are. In his mind, things are probably perfect between the two of you. He doesn't realize that you need to be reminded again and again and again about how much he likes you."

"But what about Amy? Why did he sit with her instead of me?"

"Come on, Simone. She's his best friend. You know that. He doesn't want it to seem like he's dropping her the minute he falls for a girl. See what a nice guy he is?"

I have to admit that Cleo is giving Zack much more credit than I've ever given Darius, and for a minute I feel like a lousy friend. I also have to admit that she knows way more about all of this than I do, so I take her advice: I relax.

Rivka is back at home and has been working on a new series of photographs she hopes to place in the galleries in time for the summer crowds. Her visit with her family was difficult and emotional, but I think she's glad she did it. Mordechai took the news of Rivka's illness exactly as she expected he would.

He was calm. He was reserved. He nodded. He played with his beard. And then he went into his study and closed the door and either prayed for Rivka or just went on about his day. But the best part of Rivka's visit was the chance it provided her to patch things up with her sister Devorah. Since that afternoon on the way home from the hospital, she's talked with Devorah every day, and they've made a plan for Devorah to come to Wellfleet for a few nights.

She sounds happy to be home. Happy to be working. Happy to sit in her kitchen and watch for the first signs of spring. I ask her when her next visit to Beth Israel is scheduled for.

"Never."

"What does that mean?"

"It means I just can't face another night in that hospital. I don't want to go back."

"You don't need to go back?"

"No. I said I don't want to go back. This is where I want to be. There's a hospital here. Certainly not as renowned as any of the Boston hospitals, and okay, maybe the doctors got their degrees over the Internet, but I can get the medicine and the monitoring I need on an outpatient basis."

"Well, then, I'll have to come down to see you there. Do they have a Pho Pasteur in Wellfleet?"

"No. The Briar Patch is as good as it gets. Listen, I

was thinking you could come for Passover. It's only a few weeks away. I'll do the first-night seder here. You could come with your parents and Jake, and you could even bring Zack."

I need help. I need a tutorial. I don't really understand what Passover is. I don't really understand what a seder is. I know that Passover happens sometime around Easter, but I don't think they have anything to do with each other. I don't think there are any bunnies hopping down the bunny trail at Passover. So I call Zack. I tell him, "I need help."

He sounds delighted to hear my voice. I try to sound casual, but when I hang up the phone I actually jump up and down.

Then I collapse into my chair with a huge smile on my face, his last words lingering in my head: *Lucky for you, Simone, you have me. I'll be right over.*

We're lying on my bed up in the attic. Fully clothed. On top of the covers. My dad is downstairs in the kitchen. It's late afternoon. Zack's playing with my hair.

"What's Passover exactly?" I ask.

"I knew it would come to this. I knew you were only after my wealth of Jewish knowledge."

"Well, you were bar mitzvahed, weren't you?"

241

"Indeed I was."

"Rivka invited us for Passover. Me and my family. She said she's going to do the first-night seder. For some reason I couldn't bring myself to ask her to explain it to me. She just assumed I knew all about Passover and seders."

"Passover lasts for eight days, but typically you would have a seder on the first two nights."

"What is it with the Jews and these eight-day holidays?"

"I don't know. Good question. Anyway, at a Passover seder you tell the story of the liberation of the Jews. How we were slaves in Egypt, and then Moses said, 'Let my people go,' and we wandered for forty years in the desert, and there wasn't enough time to finish baking the bread, and that's why you eat matzah, and also you eat bitter herbs to remember the bitterness of slavery."

"I'm sorry. Was that story supposed to make any sense?"

"It's complicated."

"I think that means you can't really answer my question."

"I've been celebrating Passover every year of my life."

"Well, then, can you try for a more coherent explanation?"

"I guess I need to brush up."

I stop for a minute and think about whether I'm ready to ask him my next question.

"Will you come to Rivka's with me? She told me to invite you. You made quite an impression on her."

"I'd love to. I have to run it by my parents, though. It's kind of an important family holiday in my house in spite of my lame grasp of its actual meaning. But really, I mean it, I'd love to go with you."

Zack stays for dinner. Dad has tried to make it look as if he didn't make a special effort. He brings out a big bowl of pasta with peppers and chicken sausages, and an arugula salad. Jake is out tonight at a meeting about a group project for social studies. So with Zack in Jake's seat and Mom and Dad at either end of the table, it almost feels like we're on a double date with my parents. That sounds like it would be painfully awkward, but Zack just seems to have a way with everybody. We talk and laugh, and Dad doesn't make any of his stupid jokes, and they don't grill Zack with questions, and it's just a really nice evening.

Then Mom and Dad go to clean up, and Zack gathers his books. I sit next to him on the couch as he zips up his bag.

"You know," I say, "I feel like we've done nothing but talk about me and my family situation, and I don't really know much about your family other than that your brother's name is Jesse and that you pretended you had to go visit him rather than go to James's birthday party with me."

"I'll show you the pictures from my weekend. I have proof. And anyway, your story is far more interesting than mine. That's why we talk about it."

"You mean you don't have any pregnant Hasidic teenagers lurking in your family tree?"

"No. Just a boring old mom and dad who met in college and have been married twenty-three years. You should come meet them. Maybe this weekend. But I'm warning you, my dad can't cook."

"What about your mom?"

"She's even worse than Dad."

I take his hand and put my palm up against his. His fingers are long and skinny. He intertwines them with mine. "Come on," I say. "There must be something dark in your past."

"Okay. Are you ready? I used to play the electric bass. I thought I could join a punk rock band. I contemplated getting a mohawk."

"What happened?"

"I was really, really bad. Too bad even to play punk rock music. And I don't know if you've noticed, but my hair is just too good to butcher like that."

*　　*　　*

I walk him to his car. We stand in the freezing cold with our bodies pressed together. His lips are cold, but his mouth is warm and he tastes a little salty. I could stand here like this all night. He finally pulls away and gets into his car and gives one last wave and then drives off. I wrap my arms around myself and look up at the stars. The sky is filled with them. There are more stars to see than sky tonight. I think about how I used to look at a sky like this and it would make me feel small and insignificant. And tonight, as I look at the stars, I realize that I am starting to know my place among them.

twenty-one

IT'S ONLY ABOUT TEN DAYS UNTIL PASSOVER when Rivka calls to say that she can't do it. She tries to tell me that she's just really busy and she doesn't think she can get it together but when I press her she finally admits that she isn't well enough. She's exhausted. Twenty minutes on her feet sends her to bed for two hours. Too much work goes into making a seder, and Rivka reluctantly has accepted that she just isn't up to the task.

"Why don't we have it here? I'll do it. You won't have to lift a finger."

"That's really sweet of you. But come on, Simone. You don't have to do this. You can't do this. What do you know about Passover?"

"You'd be surprised. I'm a quick study. Anyway, it's settled. You're coming here. Someone will come get you, so you don't have to worry about driving."

"I'm not really driving anymore. Doctor's orders. But if you wouldn't mind another guest, I'm sure I could get a friend to bring me up."

"Bring as many friends as you want. It's a holiday. We should have a house filled with family and friends."

I realize that I've just offered up our home, and by default Dad's services in the kitchen, because—who am I kidding?—I can't cook. I certainly can't cook for a crowd.

I'd better run this by the parents.

Mom and Dad are sitting out on the porch. It's just warm enough that with a sweater and a coat and a mug of something hot to drink, sitting outside is a pleasure. I know that they're the ones who pushed me to call Rivka, to spend time with her, but I wonder if maybe I haven't crossed the line. I just invited Rivka and her friends here for Passover. I've volunteered to have a seder in the home of my devoutly atheist parents.

"Hi, guys."

"Hey, kiddo. Do you want some hot chocolate?" asks Dad.

"No, thanks." I sit on the bench next to Mom and put my feet up on the table. "About Passover . . ."

"Oh, right. That's coming up, isn't it?"

"Yeah. But Rivka can't do it. She isn't feeling up to it."

"Oh, honey. I'm sorry." Mom puts her hand on my knee.

"So I offered our house. I told Rivka she could come up here with some friends and that we would do a seder. I'll be in charge, I promise. I'll figure out what we need to do."

They look at each other.

"I really want to do this for her. This is important to me."

Dad gets up and squeezes himself onto the bench so that I am wedged in between them. They both put their arms around me.

"Are you up for this?" asks Dad. "This may not be easy." I know he means more than just putting on the seder. I nod and rest my head on his shoulder.

Zack and I don't see that much of each other at school, and I've stopped reading too much into this. Our schedules are just incompatible. I've also stopped waiting for him to break up with me. I've stopped waiting for him to tell me that he can't help that he loves Amy Flannigan even though she already has a boyfriend. I've started to just enjoy that something really nice is happening between us.

Today we have a rare free period together. We find a corner of the library with a couch and not too many people around, and again we pretend to do homework, but instead Zack has his arm around me and we just talk. Zack has volunteered to help me with the seder. His parents and his brother are going to come. Rivka is driving up with the three friends we met in the hospital. That makes a total of twelve people.

"Thirteen," says Zack.

"No, twelve."

"No, thirteen when you count Elijah."

"Who's Elijah?"

"Oh, Simone. You still have so much to learn."

I smack his hand. "Don't patronize me."

"Okay. Elijah is a prophet. You set a place for him and pour him a glass of wine, and he's supposed to visit your home during the seder."

"Well, then, I guess I'd better add one more for the shopping list."

Zack suggests that we go see the rabbi who bar mitzvahed him to get some advice and instruction. I remind Zack that places of worship give me the creeps and that I don't really relate to men of the cloth, be they priests or rabbis or monks.

"Don't worry. You'll dig Rabbi Klein. He's really cool. And I think we're in over our heads. We could use his help. I mean, we could just go talk to my dad and let him help us, but then we'd wind up with the same old seder my dad does every year. It would be more fun to do it on our own. I think Rivka would appreciate that."

I could just kiss him.

We have an appointment with Rabbi Klein a few days later. When Zack tells me that he's the rabbi at Temple Isaiah, I remember him from the town seal protest back in October. I remember how he was bald with a close-shaved beard. I remember how eloquently he spoke about the importance of keeping religion, any and all religion, out of public life. Maybe Zack is right. Maybe I will dig this Rabbi Klein.

When we arrive, he embraces Zack and musses his hair as if he were still a child. Zack steps back and puts his arm around me and says, "I'd like you to meet my girlfriend, Simone."

My girlfriend, Simone.

I shake the rabbi's hand. He seems just like a normal guy. I don't really know what I expected. Certainly not a black shirt and white collar. I know enough to know that that uniform doesn't belong in a synagogue. But I guess I expected some kind of overt sign that he's a rabbi, a holy man, not just an average-looking middle-aged white guy with dark Levi's, brown leather shoes, and a green button-down that looks like it came from Banana Republic.

He sits behind his big wooden desk, and we take the two chairs facing him. Zack says, "Simone and I are hosting our first seder and we need some guidance, because I've never led a seder and Simone has never even been to one."

The rabbi looks at me quizzically.

"I'm an atheist," I offer.

"I see."

"I'm uncomfortable with the idea of God."

"Well, then, Passover is the perfect holiday for you."

"How's that?"

"Because it is really about liberation. It commemorates the freeing of our people from enslavement. And it provides an opportunity to focus on other people in the world who are not free. That is something even the most nonreligious and even antireligious Jew can relate to."

"What about people who aren't even sure if they're really Jewish or not?"

Again that quizzical look.

Maybe it's the quiet of this office, maybe it's having Zack next to me holding my hand, maybe it's the kindness in his eyes, but for some reason I take this look as an invitation to tell Rabbi Klein the entire story of Rivka and me.

I'm feeling like I'm hanging by a thread when I get

to the end, when I get to the part about Rivka getting sicker and sicker.

"Simone," he says, "this act of yours, this wish to provide Rivka with a seder when she is too weak to create her own, is a true act of kindness and grace. It may take you a lifetime to decide if you're Jewish or not, but I will tell you that what you are doing by having this seder and inviting Rivka and her friends into your home is an act rooted in the basic tenets of Judaism. You are performing a good deed, a mitzvah, worthy of the most divine soul."

That's it. I put my face in my hands and sob. My fingers and palms are wet with tears. Zack slides his chair closer and gently rubs my back.

"I'm so sorry," I say. "I really didn't mean for this to happen. This isn't why we're here."

"There doesn't have to be only one item on our agenda today, my dear."

"She's only thirty-three."

"It is a tragedy."

"Why? Why does this happen? I mean, you must have a better understanding than almost anyone. Why would God do this?"

"I don't know."

"And you're comfortable with that?" This comes out sounding like more of an accusation than I intend.

"I have to be."

"Well, there you go. This is why religion makes no sense to me." I take a tissue from a box on his desk. "At least Christians believe in an afterlife. At least they have the luxury of pretending that when you die you go someplace better."

"For what it's worth, Simone, I believe that you are giving Rivka the gift of an afterlife."

"You mean by passing down her genes?"

"No. I mean by remembering her. I believe that is how we all live on after this life. By being remembered by those who knew and loved us. Every time you speak of Rivka after she's gone, every time you tell a story about her, every time you think of her, imagine her, for that moment she is living on. It isn't about genetics. If you had never come to know her, I wouldn't be telling you this, even though her physical traits may be passed down to your children. We are made of much more than our genes. I would imagine, Simone, that you understand this better than most."

In spite of my breakdown, we manage to leave Temple Isaiah with advice and instruction from Rabbi Klein about how to conduct our seder. He has loaned us a stack of Haggadahs, these little pamphlets you read from during the seder that tell the

Passover story. And he's given us a few articles about modern-day slavery because he says that during the seder, when we taste the bitter herbs and dip the parsley in the salt water to remind us of shed tears, it is important to think of the terrible injustices that happen in the world today, right now, all around us, and to think about what we might be able to do to repair and heal the world.

We talked about the seder plate and all the things that need to go on it, including, among other things, a lamb shank bone, which I find kind of nasty. But I put a lamb shank bone on my shopping list. We talked about the wine (did you know that each participant is expected to drink four cups of wine throughout the course of the seder?) and the matzah and the songs to sing. He wishes us luck and asks that in return for his taking the time to meet with us we promise to come back and tell him all about the evening.

When I get home I do some more Internet research on Passover. Here's what I learn: I was wrong about Easter and Passover having nothing to do with each other. Jesus was celebrating Passover when he was crucified. The Last Supper wasn't just a regular meal Jesus was having with a group of friends. The Last Supper was a Passover seder.

twenty-two

EVEN ASSUMING ELIJAH fails to make an appearance, there is no denying that we are having a huge Passover seder. What was originally going to be a party of twelve has ballooned into a party of eighteen. So if Elijah does show, that makes a total of nineteen—eighteen people and one prophet crowded around our dinner table. The more Zack and I worked on preparing for the seder and the more we talked about it, the more the people who watched us preparing started to take an interest in the evening, and soon enough everyone was inviting themselves over.

First it was Cleo, which really means Cleo *and* Darius. Mom and Dad said we should include Jules. Jake asked if Sam could come. James said he wanted in. And then Zack told me that Amy Flannigan was hoping she could join us too. So there you have it.

Poor Dad has his work cut out for him, but he seems to be enjoying the dual challenge of cooking for so many and of not using any leavened products such as bread, pasta, or pretty much anything containing flour. Remember? You eat matzah during Passover because the Jews didn't have time to finish baking the bread before they fled from Egypt. Anyway, we've cleared the living room of all the furniture and moved in the dining room table and a few folding tables from the garage, creating a large rectangle around which all eighteen of us and even Elijah will fit.

Zack has been here all afternoon. Everyone else is just arriving. His parents and his brother, Jesse, who looks almost nothing like Zack, are at the door. Jesse gives me a hug that literally lifts me up off my feet. He plants big loud kisses on both of my cheeks as if we've known each other forever. Mom whisks Zack's parents into the kitchen to meet Dad. I take another check of the table.

Everything is set. The seder plate is ready. It has the matzah, the bitter herbs, the roasted egg, the haroset (chopped-up apples and nuts and wine that is supposed to signify the mortar that the slaves of Egypt used while in servitude, or something like that), parsley, a dish of salt water, and the dreaded lamb shank bone, which has a symbolism so unpalatable to me that I'm going to let you look that one up yourself.

I've also placed an orange on the seder plate because I read a story about an old Orthodox rabbi whose reaction to the news that the Reform movement was to begin ordaining female rabbis was this: "Women belong in the rabbinate like an orange belongs on the Seder plate." I think Rivka will approve. And I'm right. She smiles the minute she sees it.

She has arrived with her friends Lila, Elena, and Val, the long-haired man who I mistook for a woman back in the hospital. You'd think if you were a man and your name was Val you might go out of your way to cultivate a look of masculinity, but apparently Val doesn't have this concern.

Rivka looks thin, pale, tired, even—and I hate to admit it—sick. But to me she still looks extraordinarily beautiful.

The house is buzzing with family, with friends, with life. Rivka and I step out onto the porch.

"What do you think?" I ask. "Did we overdo it? Are there too many people here?"

"No, no," she says. "This is exactly how it should be. This is perfect."

"You look good."

"You're lying."

"No, I mean it. I think you're beautiful."

Rivka takes a strand of my hair and tucks it behind my ear. She takes a long look at my face. "Simone," she says, "you're an angel. You make me question how I ever could have questioned my faith, because looking at you, I just can't believe that there isn't a God and that he didn't conspire to send you to me at the very moment when I most needed an angel in my life."

I'm not sure what to say. And even if I tried to speak, I don't think words would come out. I think I would open my mouth and out would come a big howling wail, and I'm not sure I would be able to stop.

"Come on," says Rivka. "Let's go inside." She takes my hand. "It's time."

If I wasn't already in love with Zack, which I am, I would fall for him hard tonight. He commands the attention of everyone in the room. He leads the group through the seder and explains each stage of the evening for those people who have never taken part in a seder before, which is the overwhelming majority of the group. He keeps bringing the conversation back from the ancient past to the present. I'm proud to be seated beside him.

We come to a part in the seder when the youngest

child is supposed to ask the Four Questions. Since there's no child at our Passover table, this duty falls to my little brother, Jake, who is the youngest among us and who seems irritated that this fact has to be pointed out to everyone. I don't care what Jake thinks. To me, in many ways, he will always be the little boy with blond curls, a freckled nose, and Bugs Bunny teeth, even though tonight there is no denying that he has become a stunning young man. As he stands up to speak I could almost fall out of my chair with the force of the love I feel for him. The questions Jake reads from the Haggadah ask why this night is different from all other nights. Why we do we eat matzah? Why do we eat bitter herbs? Why do we dip greens into salt water? And so on. But to me the answer to the principal question, the question of why this night is different from all other nights, is crystal clear. Just take a good look around this table.

There are mothers and fathers. There are sons and daughters. There are brothers and sisters. There are friends who are like brothers and sisters to each other. There is every configuration of family you can imagine.

I think again about family trees. I think of Rivka's and how it includes Mordechai and Hannah and all her siblings, and then there is an offshoot that includes me, and by extension Jake and Mom and Dad, and then it curves around with more branches for her friends like Lila and Elena and Val.

I think about my family tree. I think about how wrong I was for all those years to imagine it as bare.

epilogue

RIVKA DIED AT THE END OF APRIL, just after I turned seventeen. She died at home, in her beloved house in Wellfleet, with her friends and even some family around her. I was there. So was her sister Devorah. Even though we were all prepared for that day, even though we knew it was coming, in the end nothing could have prepared me for it. I'm still trying to make sense of it, of watching the life go out of someone so full of life. Forgive me, but this is all I can say about that day.

She was buried the next morning down the road from her house. A small group of us gathered to say goodbye. With the help of Zack and Rabbi Klein, I was able to recite the Kaddish at her grave site, the Jewish prayer for the dead. This isn't something that would have been appreciated by Mordechai had he been present. Traditionally, the Kaddish is recited by a man, and many consider it a disadvantage if you bear no sons because you won't have a child who can recite the Kaddish for you when you die. But Mordechai was not there. And Rivka had me, her daughter. I was able to stand at her grave and recite the Kaddish and say, "*Aleha ha-shalom.*"

Mordechai marked Rivka's death in the way he knew how. He sat shiva for a week in his home, in the company of his surviving children, receiving a steady stream of visitors from within his community. And on the third day of the shiva I appeared.

This wasn't the shocker you might imagine. It wasn't one of those moments of loud gasps or dropping jaws. I walked in, properly attired in a long skirt, and walked right up to Mordechai. He was sitting in a chair, his hands folded in his lap. He looked just like the pictures I have of him, although his beard was finally starting to show some gray. I pulled up a chair and sat down facing him.

"I want to introduce myself," I said.

"There is no need. I know who you are."

This caught me off guard. I didn't know what to say.

"You look just like her," he said.

I let this sink in. "I'm sorry for your loss."

"And I am sorry for yours."

And that was it. What else did I have to say to this

man, who also happens to be my grandfather? That I'm sorry for my loss too? That I'm sorry that I lost Rivka after knowing her for such a brief time? That I'm sorry that I lost out on the chance to have known her from the very beginning?

I took a quick look around the house. I even snuck upstairs and found the room I imagine Rivka slept in with her sisters. I looked at the neatly made bed (only one in the room, although back then there must have been three) and thought of Rivka as a sixteen-year-old girl lying there in the dark, staring at the ceiling, broken from the callousness of a boy named Joe and terrified by the strange and mysterious changes happening inside of her.

I went back downstairs and talked briefly with Devorah. I watched as all of the other Levin children and their families either ignored me because they had no idea who I was or ignored me because they knew precisely who I was.

As I was getting ready to leave I went to find Mordechai again. He was alone in the kitchen, staring out the back window. I wasn't finished with him yet.

"How long have you known about me?"

"I knew," he said.

"You knew then? You knew when she was pregnant?"

"Of course."

"Why didn't you do anything? Why didn't you say anything to her?"

"Because I loved her more than anything."

"That isn't how she saw it. She felt abandoned by you."

"That is unfortunate."

"Yes. It is."

"I had no choice."

"You always have a choice. Life is nothing but what happens as a result of all your choices."

"If that is so, then I think I've made the right ones."

I looked at his hands. They were big and thick and perfectly still at his sides. Mine, I noticed, were trembling.

"With all due respect, Rabbi, I disagree."

"That is your choice."

And now we were really through. I turned around, walked away and out of the Rebbe's house, and drove back home. I'd be lying if I didn't tell you that there was a small part of me that imagined I might have some tearful reunion with this man. That we would see something in common between us, and carve out some kind of grandfather/granddaughter relationship. But I know now what a fantasy this was. A childish fantasy. I've learned enough this year to know that life may surprise you, but not usually in the ways you imagine.

I managed to get through the end of the school year with respectable grades. All that studying of my vocabulary words paid off. I aced the SAT. I should get to go to the college of my choice. At least that's what Mr. McAdams tells me.

Zack worked at the Organic Oasis all summer and also interned for Rabbi Klein at Temple Isaiah. I worked at the city day camp in Boston. We still had weekends and some nights to be together, and we took advantage of every opportunity we had. Cleo and Darius broke up. She found out about another party and another girl, and this time his tears did nothing for her. Even though I saw this coming from day one, I took no pleasure in being proved right. I ached for Cleo. It was a really rough summer for her, but she's finally back to herself now.

School starts again in two weeks, and I'm looking forward to my senior year. To having more time with Zack. To watching Jake play varsity soccer. To seeing what happens next with Cleo. To my new position as features editor on the *Gazette*. But not to my role in the Atheist Student Alliance. I plan to resign as soon as school starts. It's not like I've found God or religion, but here's what I've come to realize: I'm not a real atheist. I don't think I ever was. That's who Mom and Dad are, and I love them for it. But there's too much that I don't understand or can't explain, and I don't have an unshakable belief in the absence of a higher power. For me, there are still too many questions, and I am just beginning a long search for the answers.

And tonight I'm with my family. We're spending the weekend in Wellfleet in the little pink house with the crushed-stone driveway and the porch with the view of the water that now belongs to me.

The summer heat is just starting to fade. This evening the yard is filled with the sounds of birds darting in and out of the pine trees. It's Friday night. And because this house was so much a part of Rivka, tonight, before we sit down to Dad's elaborate dinner at the old wooden table, we light candles and drink wine and eat challah. We stumble our way through the blessings, surrounded by all of her things.

Rivka replaced the photograph above the fireplace with a new one from her final series. I think it's the same beach. The same spot with the sea and the sand and the grass. But this picture is taken at the end of a day, and instead of being filled with movement, this picture is still. Quiet. Peaceful.

I step outside after dinner and take in a deep

breath of the salty sea air. I look up at the sky that is just turning dark and just revealing its stars. I think of Rivka. I picture her sitting in her kitchen. I imagine her standing on her front porch. I think of Rivka. I picture Rivka. I imagine Rivka.

I remember her.

acknowledgments

Thank you

To my dear friend and agent, Douglas Stewart, for more than there is room to say on this page.

To Wendy Lamb, for believing in me and this book and for never losing enthusiasm for this story even after reading it again and again and again.

To my family for their support and encouragement, particularly Mary Lelewer and Ann Sokatch, who read these pages almost as quickly as they were written.

To Brendan Halpin for his invaluable insights and for keeping me entertained with his e-mails and the latest installments from his wonderful novels.

To Noa Stolzenberg-Myers, my first young reader, for spending her summer vacation with an early draft of this book.

And finally to my loving husband and avid reader, Daniel Sokatch, who did nothing but cheer me on and was kind enough not to pester me about getting a real job while I was busy writing this story.

about the author

DANA REINHARDT lives in Los Angeles with her husband and their two children. This is her first book.
Visit her online at www.danareinhardt.net